The Life and Dreams of Pimientos de Padrón

Katherine Anne Lee

1st Vintage Book Edition

© 09.2014 KAL - Katherine Anne Lee
Author: Katherine Anne Lee, Switzerland
Lector: Christopher J. Lee, Switzerland
Illustration design: Ilona Mulock Houwer, Belgium

ISBN   978-3-9524205-6-0

www.katherine-anne-lee.com

Chapters

Introduction to a faraway place

This is a story that takes you to a faraway place. I'd like to give you the opportunity to escape this planet for a while and let your thoughts wander. You know, dive into an unreal world where so much more is possible, and innocence truly lives. Take a deep breath. Imagine the image. Taste the sweetness of the being.

But is such a world really so unreal?

Have we traded our innocence?

Do we hide away soft feelings on purpose?

For a moment, let's imagine a normal day in a normal life. Does the day start before the sun even touches the outer walls of our home?

Are we caught up with getting up on time? Trying not to forget the hands of time that keep ticking on, while hot water washes away the nightmares of our restless sleep. Do we dash onto a bus or the underground, and dodge familiar faces to avoid speaking about our lives?

We work all day under a dull light, and then rush off to pick up dinner and the dry cleaning. Finally, back home again, we flake out on the couch after eating too quickly. Feeling disturbed by, but at the same time strangely enchained to the flickering pictures on our television. Once the clock surprisingly strikes too many times, we stagger off to bed after too much wine. The rhythm repeats itself, and the nightmares don't go away.

At this moment in life, it may be time to ask a simple question. What is the reason for my life?

What do I want to be?

What's my goal, and how would I like to be remembered?

There's no general answer that fits everything, and this is not a guidebook. There's no step one, two or three. Every reason for being is very individual, and the same applies to the purpose, as well as the journey to find it.

My main characters in this story serve as a proxy, and will hopefully spark some unconscious inspiration. Let's just enjoy a fun story and allow our thoughts to form without even noticing. So, please pack your imaginary bags. You won't need a lot. We're off to a sunny corner of this planet with fertile land, offering nearly everything and everybody the opportunity to grow. The country of our destination nourishes the hopes and dreams of many, as well as those of Pimientos de Padrón.

I know we've only just started, but you're probably asking yourself what Pimientos de Padrón are. Well... I would have asked myself the same question a few years ago. I was introduced to the little fellas in a tapas bar in Spain, on the island of Majorca to be exact.

They are thumb-size green peppers that are fried in high quality olive oil for a few minutes. Once they've become a bit sloppy looking, I guess you could call it a dark army-green, they are presented on a plate and well salted with Fleur de

Sel or a similar gourmet salt. It's a typical dish that you put in the middle of the table, and everybody just helps themselves to these little green snacks.

Let me add that you don't eat them with a knife and fork. No, you just pick them up by the stem and bite off their delicious bodies.

I was immediately addicted, and being a salt lover only supported my newly found drug. We travelled the island, and I soon found that I was choosing restaurants that serve this dish. My craving was further nourished as we ended our holidays in Madrid. And let me tell you, that city has a tapas bar on every corner. This made it easy for me to still my hunger.

Back home, my newly trained eye for Pimientos de Padrón soon found out that the little old town speciality grocers, just two minutes from where we live, actually sell the peppers. This information probably makes it easy for you to guess what I do every Saturday. And yes, you're spot on. I have learned to make them myself.

"One day you will turn into a Pimiento de Padrón," my husband warned me. This sentence was the start of the tale of "The Life and Dreams of Pimientos de Padrón".

It made me think about what I want to achieve in life.

What is the higher goal for us humans?

What do you want to be?

What do you want to become?

How do you see yourself, and how do you think people in your surroundings would describe you?

To nourish the thought in a simpler way, I asked myself, "what do these green peppers want in life?", and this fantasy tale is the answer I came up with.

One little warning before we get back to the actual story. On every plate of Pimientos de Padrón you will always have one hot, and I mean really hot pepper. You can't tell which one it is until you've chewed on it. It's like the wolf dressed as the grandmother in Little Red Riding Hood. You never know what you're getting until it's too late.

So lean back and let the wind sweep you away to the land of the hopes and dreams of Pimientos de Padrón.

Our soul's birth 1

Our travel to a fruitful land begins. Like a leaf that's survived the mild winter and been ungratefully let go by its tree, you're sailing freely through the air. Now look down. What do you see in this faraway land?

You are looking at acres and acres of hilly, prosperous land beneath you. Winter has just ended, and silver lining of morning dew covers the hills. Well, winter is actually not the right word to use in this corner of the world - the temperature never really drops below zero. But they do have four seasons, and winter is the official name for this time of the year.

As soon as the sun touches the earth, the ground turns a dark, chocolate-brown colour. Nothing is growing yet, and while you sail through the crisp air, you can hear an engine starting up in the distance.

It's seven in the morning, and Farmer Gonzales has started his working day. Fifteen minutes later, his red tractor is running up and down the hills, turning the fruitful ground, getting ready for the next week's seeding session.

By the late afternoon and after a short sandwich picnic under an old oak tree, Farmer Gonzales finishes his last field. They are now all symmetrically combed in one direction. From above, the picture could be from a postcard. Like the lavender fields you see in the South of France, just a darker colour.

As the day ends, the evening sun dyes the scenery into an orangey-brown picture, with the old oak tree as the only green spot. Above, the stars come out in the dark blue sky, and start to twinkle in expectation of what's to come.

As the night fully takes over, the land quietens, and, one by one, the farmhouses turn off their lights.

In their barn, the seeds of the country's future plants rustle in excitement. They are the souls of the land, the souls of Pimientos de Padrón. For generations they have been planted, have grown and have given birth to plants and their peppers. Their constant rebirth has allowed them to experience the evolution of life, one decade after another. The knowledge they store is exceptional, and there's not an area of life they're not taught about.

*****

The heavy seed bags, which only a strong man can lift, lean against each other in rows. Inside the gunny sacks, the seeds of life rub against each other with a rhythmic melody. They sing tales of past lives, their hopes for the future, their luscious green leaves and the most enchanting flowers that will grow from their pod. It's their destiny to be the most beautiful, weather-resistant home to the future Padróns. They will play their role in life perfectly, to ensure that the peppers become plump vegetables with shiny coats. Their veins give life to others, and transport the nourishment and knowledge needed. This is their purpose, their reason for being.

Inside the bags of life, it's like being in a cave filled with believers; moon, or even planet worshipers dancing to the single rhythm of a drum. Moving in the same direction, stretching their arms into the air and praising life. Their stamping feet raise the red dust with every beat.

The heat rises, and their damp bodies reflect the low light that finds its way into their cave. The air is filled with a salty taste, mixed with the smell of wood and churned sand. Moving up and down and swirling around, they churn against each other.

Souls find souls and dance together to the rhythm of the music. Every movement tells a tale of life and its purpose.

The beat of the drums increases, a gush of soft sand swirls through the air and strokes the souls' bodies. The pace of the rhythm accelerates. Heat rises and the tension becomes unbearable as the seeds exchange quick movements.

At first, only single shouts of joy escape the lips of some, but soon the whole crowd stretches its arms to the sky and screams in excitement.

In anticipation, they long for the moment when they will be set free in one of the fields, and the damp ground will embrace their bodies. That will be the moment when their shells can give way to the growing pressure inside them. They will crack open and life will spill out. Their souls will be free, and there will be no turning back anymore. Their path to destiny will soon open up in front of them.

The next drum beats calm the crowd and takes them into a smoother state of trance. The movements slow down and their breathing catches up again, as they sway against each other in perfect harmony, gathering strength for the next peak to come.

Their songs and prayers do not go unheard. They are not alone in the farmer's barn. As soon as all has gone quiet outside, the corn mice leave their safe homes.

For years they have lived in the farm's storage areas. Generation after generation has grown up in the sheds, and have profited from the wealth of food. Their nests are cosy and warm, and some are dug far down into the ground. Tunnels link their nests to each other, allowing a healthy social environment.

Not all are happy about their presence, however. The measures taken to thin down their population may have been successful, but their large ears and black eyes serve them well. They have also worked out crafty strategies of how to trick the farmer's cats.

Grouped together, they agree on a plan before leaving their sheltered homes. Divided into groups and with a designated lookout, they leave their holes. First the guards get into position. Once they are sure the air is clear, signals are given to the waiting groups. One by one they scatter out and run across the floor of the barn to form their groups. Tonight there are three troops. The first group will attack from the left side. The second group from the right and the third group, well the third group are the grenadiers, which means the toughest of mice, who will go straight towards the desired treats.

The left and right group quickly run along the walls of the barn. Every now and then the leader slows down, looks left, right and back to the guards. All is according to plan - they quickly scurry on.

The grenadiers sneak across the middle of the room and split into three small sub-groups. The commander of each sub-group makes signs to his followers with his tail. Step by step they sneak across the clay floor. Every ten steps, the tough mice crouch down and lay their heads on the cool ground, while the commander checks their position. The barn is quiet. Only the light tiptoeing sound of their friends and family mice running along the walls can be heard. A dusty wood scent lies in the air, and, through a crack in the wall, a little moonlight shines into the barn and onto the ground. There are no other movements.

Once everything is clear, they run on until they reach their target. Gathered around one gunny sack filled with seeds, they split up once more, and the commander sends his soldiers to find points of easy access. The mice scramble up the gunny sacks. Up and down they run. Their light footsteps join the beats of the seeds, massaging the bags inside, but no opening is found.

The smell of the grains is enchanting, and not all the mice can resist. One young grenadier is overwhelmed. The heavenly scent fills his nostrils, and the full bag beneath his feet is just too much. He can't stop himself anymore, he turns onto his back and rubs himself against the gunny sack. The scent intensifies, and he closes his eyes and lets his thoughts go. In fantasy, he is lying on a bed of grain with the most beautiful lady mice admiring him. Stretching his arms and legs, he loses his position, and, before he knows what's happening, he's hurtling down the sack. With horror, he can see the ground and his commander coming closer, but there's nothing he can do to stop his fall. With a muffled bump he lands on the clay. Everything goes black, and small stars blind his view.

After a split second of shock, the grenadiers know they must act quickly. He is immediately picked up by two colleagues and carried back to their home. The last thing he sees before leaving the scene is the stabbing look of his commander. He has endangered the group.

Back at the gunny sacks, a group of mice meet at the corner of one bag. On command, they attack the material, and, taking turns, they bite and chew. Their hard work is soon rewarded with the spilling of seeds onto the shed's cool, clay floor. Hundreds of souls lie scattered across the ground. The mice quickly fill their mouths and run back and forth between their homes and the sacks. This is the most dangerous part of the operation. The excitement is high, and the intense smell of seeds is enchanting. The guards' eyes dart around the barn, and - there they are! The twinkling eyes of their biggest enemy, the farmer's cat. The commander immediately sounds the alarm, and every mouse runs for safety. The ones too far away from home have no choice but to hide between the gunny sacks and wait for their moment to run across the floor. But the farmer's cat is quick and knows no mercy. Not all of them will make it home tonight.

One white mouse overestimates his sprinting prowess. With one swipe of the cat's paw he's thrown into the corner like a squash ball. Now the cat starts its game, with the dizzy white mouse as his plaything.

The nightmare of one is survival for the others. Taking advantage of the situation, the other mice run back to their holes. This night is a feast for some, and their larders are filled for days to come.

Even if hundreds of seeds spill, and souls are lost forever, there are still thousands left who will find their destiny in one of the fields. It's not meant for every soul to be born. Some stay as souls forever, and never advance to a real life on our earth. Their meaning of life is of a different kind, and is not always evident. Only the very fortunate will make their way forward, and blossom on our planet.

The moon makes its way across the night sky, while, inside the barn, one mouse gives his life for others to fill their stomachs and rest peacefully in their safe nests in the land of the hopes and dreams of Pimientos de Padrón.

Deepening
our roots

2

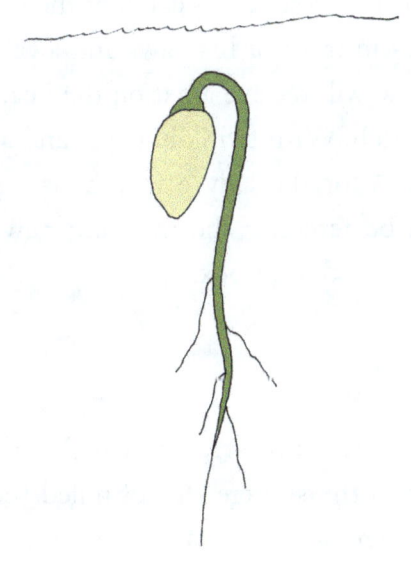

The next day, the sun rises early. Its warmth is increasing with every day as summer draws closer. The mice rest comfortably inside their safe homes. Their filled tummies gently rise up and down with every breath while they lie cuddled up together in their warm nests. A peaceful atmosphere surrounds them. Their existence is secured for days to come.

Outside, in front of the farmer's home, the cat proudly sits on the doorstep and presents his catch of the night. One dead white mouse lies in front of his paws and awaits recognition. He knows that he will receive a pat on the head and a special treat for every catch. With twinkling eyes and a straight back, he patiently waits for the lady of the house to awaken. He knows she will be fetching the morning newspaper that is dangling from the red letterbox.

*****

Farmer Gonzales is up early as usual. After a quick cup of coffee, he inspects the storage shed. Spilled seeds across the floor of the barn are not an unusual sight. But it nevertheless makes him shake his head every time. He quickly sweeps all the spilt seeds together with a brush, and puts them into a new gunny sack. His strong brother is supporting him today, helping to get his machinery ready for the seeding season.

Together they lift the heavy sacks onto their shoulders, carry them out into the open and empty them into a large funnel on the back of his red tractor. When the first load is ready to go, the two of them sit on the porch and ease their hunger with a jam sandwich and another cup of coffee. It's going to be a long day in the fields.

Inside the funnel, the seeds are tight with anticipation. They know that they are the first souls that will be presented to the world. They will be the first to touch real soil, to suck up the earth's water and rise to the sky. But being first out also entails more danger. Early in the season, natural hazards, followed by pests, could hinder their purpose in life. Their purpose is to become strong, beautiful plants that are the home of the Pimientos de Padrón. Anxiously, they lie on top of each other and hold their breath.

Eventually, the tractor engine starts up and the funnel starts vibrating. The seeds rub against each other and start an ancient song, praising their departure. This is their last common path together.

*****

With a rattling funnel, the tractor rolls up the stony path to the fruitful fields. The combination of the heat and the rising dust inside the container is unbearable. Some of the seeds are close to passing out, when suddenly the hatch below opens for a second, letting a little air into the funnel. An automatic arm snatches one of them and the hatch immediately closes again. It all happens so fast that it's hardly noticed by the seeds lying on top.

The process repeats itself at short intervals. One by one, they are taken and carried to the outside world. The seeds bounce rhythmically on top of each other and, inch by inch, slip closer to the bottom of the funnel. Once outside, the automatic arm clutches a single seed, and buries it into the brown soil before letting go. It all happens within seconds, and, before the seed knows what's happening, brown earth is crumbling down on top of it.

Bedded in its final station, the seed sits and waits. Above, the thick earth trembles to the tractor's beat, while, from the side, the soil presses down as the automatic arm digs the next hole. The seed sits and listens as the sound of the tractor slowly disappears into the distance.

The surrounding earth is warm and damp, the ideal circumstances for growing quickly. The seed smiles to itself and waits.

A soul has been planted.

Some hours later, all has gone quiet. The tractor has left the field and is back at the farm. The soil surrounding the seed slowly cools down, and the dark surroundings turn a total black. The seed closes its eyes and sleeps peacefully. It will need all the energy it can get for the coming weeks.

*****

The next day, the seed is woken by a thumping sound above its head. Water is falling from the sky. The soil around the seed widens like a sponge and thickens. Once the earth is full and can't take anymore, small streams of water trickle past the seed. Giggling, the round pod of life turns from one side to the other, enjoying the refreshing feeling.

Above ground, the surface sprinklers are doing their work. They are settling the ground by watering the fields. The seeds shell softens as the water runs deeper and deeper.

Rays of sunlight touch the ground and warm the soil, and a damp smell fills the air. A fine line of mist rises from the ground, turning the hills into mystic places.

Far below the earth's surface, the ground bubbles. Life presses against the seed's soft shell. The increasing pressure moves the seed, and it stretches its body in agony. Squeezing its eyes closed, moaning against the ripping pain, it tries to imagine its arms digging through the soil.

A moment later, the shell cracks. The seed loudly groans and allows its insides to expand. The pressure reduces, and the seed takes a few deep breaths before falling back down into the earth's cushion. The doors have opened and its arms can grow. Satisfied, the seed leans back and rests.

An ecru-coloured, pointy head pushes its way through the opening in the seed's shell. A little unsure, it looks left and right, then up and down. All seems clear. There are no sounds to be heard, except the steady heartbeat of its soul. Beneath, the earth is thick and solid, not the direction to grow; the ecru head knows that. Above, the soil is looser and can be pushed aside. That's the direction it must go. Taking up all its courage, it slides its still-small body out of the shell and winds its head upwards between the grains of earth, which easily give way. A satisfied smile broadens on the head's face. It enjoys the feeling of soft, damp earth surrounding its newly created body. The grains stabilize its thin silhouette. It stretches itself a little more and sticks its nose into the patch of earth lying above. It smells damp, a mossy kind of fragrance. The perfect surrounding for a newly growing plant. Happy with itself, it rests its head against the mossy smelling soil and falls asleep.

In its dream, the head can see itself growing rapidly. The earth opens a gateway in front of it to make space and provide a perfect path. Feeling like a star, the head proudly dances to an ancient, elegant tune, past the grains of earth, which applaud every step it takes. It is wearing a green, bushy hat that makes it look even taller and very elegant. Around the brown carpet of fame, the earth grains crouch down and clap their hands in the air. Their eyes are filled with excitement. A new star is born. Every now and then, the head reaches for its bushy hat, takes it from its head and bows down or simply uses it as extended hand to wave to the crowd. The females scream and their wobbly knees give way. As they touch the ground, they spill across the carpet and break into hundreds of small grains. The head doesn't mind, it is the new star, and this is what it expects.

Its parade is suddenly interrupted. The earth grumbles and shakes. Brown grains start to crumble and block the head's path, spilling in front of its feet. A drilling sound gets louder and louder, while the earth continues to quake. The head is left with no choice but to press itself towards the ground to prevent being shaken all over the place. The soil around the head moves to the beat of the drill, and presses itself against the head's cheeks. The ground thickens and the drilling noise grows to an unbearable level. Something wet and slippery slides across the head's face. Startled, the soon-to-be-plant freezes in shock. A giant worm wrangles its way past. The plant tries to scream, but no sounds come out.

Short of breath, the head wakes up to find itself in exactly the same situation. It is being pushed down deeper into the ground. Its open mouth has filled with grains of earth, and its head has gone all slippery from the worm's damp body brushing across it. Squeezing its eyes closed, it's left with no choice but to pray and wait until the seemingly never-ending body passes by.

After what felt like hours, but must have only been minutes of terror, the scare is over. The drilling sound becomes more distant, and the head can move again. A little shook-up, it shakes itself and gets back into position.

Nothing is going to stop it from growing! Nothing is going to stop it fulfil its destiny of becoming a strong, beautiful plant! The home of the mighty Pimientos de Padrón - its sole purpose in life. No worm will hinder this from happening.

Determined, the head stretches itself and pushes its way through some loose grains of earth. "Ha, that'll show them," it smiles, spitting the remaining pieces of earth out of its mouth. Appreciating itself, it looks back down its long neck.

"Not bad for my first day," it winks to the grains of earth. Far below, it can see the opened brown seed, its soul, and it knows that this will be the last time it will be able to spot this pod of life. But no matter how far it will grow, it will always remain attached to its sole purpose, and the bond will feed its need for knowledge. It knows that if it keeps on growing at this speed, it will be touching the surface within days.

But the head has misjudged the effort needed. The nourishing ground supports its path by providing all the energising food needed. The sprinklers keep on dampening the earth and giving the water of life. But this alone is not enough to make the whole journey to the top. The plant has to gain muscles quickly. It has to be strong, as not all of the earth's grains are willing to be moved aside. Some of them are rock-hard and persistent about staying in their location. The head has the choice to fight, or take a detour around the obstacle. These barriers in life torment the mind and strengthen the body. This head will one day become a strong plant, ready to survive the entire unknown of the outside.

On the fifth day, it pushes the last grains of soil aside and stretches its head towards the blue sky. It has arrived. Its dark journey has ended, and it's finally in the outside world. Running sprinklers wash the brown remains from the young plant. Rays of sunlight kiss its head. Its yellowish colour will not survive very long. The sun and the wind will soon dye its head a luscious green.

While the sun sinks that evening, little water pearls sitting on the bud's head sparkle in the most beautiful red tones. From afar, the fields seem to be scattered with little rubies, reflecting the evening sun.

What a beautiful sight! What a magical scene in the land of the hopes and dreams of Pimientos de Padrón.

Our soul's essence 3

On its first day out in the open, the young plant turns his head and inspects its surrounding. On all sides it can see other young buds that, like it, have escaped the dark and entered the new world. It smiles happily to itself. It's not alone. It has companions who have fought the same fight and are now ready to face the future.

Today, the fields are brown, as far as the eye can see. But the hilly area will soon be painted a luscious green. They will be seen and admired for miles. With this positive thought, the plant takes a deep breath and stretches its head towards the rising sun. But it's not only its head that moves through this intention. Beside it, two tiny leaves lift themselves in synchrony. Amazed, the bud's head looks left and right. "I have arms," it cries out. Chuckling noises ring out. Confused, it looks around. A field of buds is looking in its direction and laughing. Ashamed, it pulls its tiny leaves closer to its body to cover whatever is there or may still be missing.

"Don't worry, we're all the same," a sweet voice sings from the left. "Stand straight, you don't want the farmer to stretch you or even tie you to a pole," it warns with a wink.

"A pole isn't that bad," says another plant, standing in the next row. "You can wriggle yourself up it and don't need to worry whether your stem's thick enough. Quite practical indeed, I've heard," it ends, nodding its head.

"Yeah, I bet. Well, I'm going to make it all by myself. No pole needed over here, I tell you," replies the plant to its left, waving its arms in a self-assured manner. "By the way, I'm CLARITY, the soul of clarity," she smiles. "Mr Lazy-Pole over there is the soul of marvellous-me, so just MARVELLOUS-ME. And who are you?" she asks with an interested expression.

"Hmmm," the young plant wonders. "I'm a plant, the future home of Pimientos de Padrón," it smiles, feeling proud and quite satisfied with its quick answer.

"Yeah, we know. We all are. But what's your name?" MARVELLOUS-ME shouts across the lane. He's starting to look bored.

Name? The plant wonders, it can't understand what they mean. "I don't have a name," it answers confused.

"Of course you do. You just have to ask for it," CLARITY calmly explains.

"Ask for it? Who do I ask?" the plant replies, wondering if it has missed something.

CLARITY and MARVELLOUS-ME exchange a funny look. "You just ask yourself. Your inner soul, your higher purpose. Try it!" CLARITY encourages. The plant squeezes its eyes closed.

"A name, a name, I need a name," it pleads to itself, but nothing happens.

"So?" CLARITY asks impatiently.

"Um, I'm Padrón," the young plant whispers, with only one eye open and crouched head as if it expected a spanking.

"No, you're not!", hits back CLARITY sharply. "You're not doing it properly. How are you ever going to find out about the world? How do you think MARVELLOUS-ME knows about the poles? Do you see any poles?" she glares at him. The young plant has no clue and just stares back at her with widened eyes.

"Huff, it's always the same. You need to ask your soul to find answers. We all do. It's easy!" she explains, while her sharp eyes burn into its young stem. "That's how our knowledge is transported from one generation to the other. The earth and the water that feed you will also nourish your thoughts with the latest news of the world. Don't worry about all that," she smiles at last. "Your soul carries all our ancestors' knowledge, you just need to go and fetch it. Now, relax, stretch yourself, feel the sun on your face and the wind touching your leaves. Calm down, feel yourself and then… then you ask," she explains with excited eyes and both of her leaves resting on her hip.

The plant takes a deep breath, closes its eyes again and stretches towards the sun. "Looking better," MARVELLOUS-ME comments, but it doesn't let the voice disturb it. It wants to find its name.

The sun is warming its whole body. With closed eyes, everything looks yellow and bright. Its mind wanders through its body. It can feel its feet digging into the ground. It is standing strong and the earth's grains are supporting it. From deep below, water is refreshing its veins. Everything is in order. It is feeling well and happy, at peace with earth. And there it is, its name …. Suddenly it knows it. "INNOCENCE, I am the soul of innocence," the plant shouts out without opening its eyes.

"So, INNOCENCE it will be," CLARITY smiles. In the distance, the farmer's tractor starts up.

"Uh, get in position guys and girls, Farmer Gonzales is on his way! We'd better look our best," CLARITY warns, while turning back to the sun and making herself look long. INNOCENCE, MARVELLOUS-ME and all the others join in. In unity, they all face the same direction and proudly present their young, immaculate bodies.

No poles will be needed today in the land of the hopes and dreams of Pimientos de Padrón.

A sense of basic trust 4

The plants grow up quickly in the hilly fields. It doesn't take long before there are only fine brown lanes left for the eye to see. The green, bushy plants catch the eye now. In perfect lines, they stand in rows, one after the other. Their creamy leaves have turned to a dark green and form a wonderful contrast to the bright blue sky above them.

It's a hot day and CLARITY, MARVELLOUS-ME and INNOCENCE long for the evening to come and for the sprinklers to set in.

"God, this heat is unbearable. I'm dripping wet," MARVELLOUS-ME moans. "What do you think? If I shake my booty like this, how far will I get? Do you think I can fling some of my wet body pearls onto your highest leaves up there?" MARVELLOUS-ME cunningly asks, with a twinkle of naughtiness in his eye.

"How dare you! You're disgusting," CLARITY pouts at him and demonstratively turns to the sun.

"Ha, if you carry on like that, you'll shrivel away to a sad little brown patch," MARVELLOUS-ME hits back, swaying his hips rhythmically. "On days like this it's all about keeping your head low, sweetie. Sneak under your neighbour's shade, if he's providing any," he shouts at the plant next to him, which just ignores him.

"You have to admit, MARVELLOUS-ME, it's difficult to shade you. Even if someone wanted to, you're too...," INNOCENCE loses his voice and stares at the ground in shock, realizing what he just wanted to say.

"I'm what?" MARVELLOUS-ME snaps. "Go on, what am I?" he insistently pushes.

"You know, you're too... err... big," INNOCENCE mumbles, chewing his lower lip.

"I've no idea what you are mumbling about. Look at me! Yes, I'm big, big and strong," says MARVELLOUS-ME, proudly stretching himself and flexing his muscles towards the sky. But his muscle-man warrior pose is too much. His centre loses balance, and suddenly all he can see are the dry crumbles of earth coming towards him at lightning speed.

"Wäähff...," buff. MARVELLOUS-ME lands mouth first in the soil of the narrow path between him, CLARITY and INNOCENCE.

"Pppfff....," CLARITY cries out in laughter while INNOCENCE looks shocked, still trying to catch up on what has just happened.

"I can't see, I can't see," cries MARVELLOUS-ME, spitting out pieces of dry soil.

"Don't worry, you are just where you deserve to be. At my feet," CLARITY splutters out laughing. "Uhh, I have a little itch on my left foot. Would you mind giving it a rub, MARVELLOUS-ME?" CLARITY teases.

"Stop laughing, you're not funny! Help me!" MARVEL-LOUS-ME commands desperately, still clearing his throat. "My eyes are blocked. It hurts," he goes on, sobbing to himself.

"Well, you're in the shade now," says INNOCENCE, trying to calm him, but actually feeling a little worried.

"Yes, look at the bright side of life, MARVELLOUS-ME, for once you are totally covered, covered in dust," CLARITY giggles.

"One of you help me! Get down here now and lend me a hand," MARVELLOUS-ME demands angrily.

INNOCENCE blinks nervously and tries to bend himself towards the ground. "Don't you do that! You'll snap in two. We're too tall for that. MARVELLOUS-ME just has to keep calm and wait. It won't be long and the sprinklers will set in. With the strength of the water, MARVELLOUS-ME's roots may be able to heave him up again." CLARITY warns.

"Huh, water! Who needs water; watch me, I don't need anybody's help," MARVELLOUS-ME protests, and gathers all his strength. He pumps all his so-called muscles, which have slumped down into his belly due to the fall, back up to his chest. "Wwrahh," MARVELLOUS-ME screams, squeezing his eyes closed. His knuckles colour red and tears run down his dusty cheeks as he manages to lift his head off the ground. His backbone curls like an electrified cat. Shivering from tip to toe, he remains in this position for a few seconds, showing off his white teeth. Saliva is running down the side of his mouth. "Ahhh," he cries and flops back down to the ground like a drowned rat. He just doesn't have the energy to lift himself back up again.

INNOCENCE nervously blinks and looks to CLARITY for help. "We've got to do something, CLARITY. He's our friend, we can't leave him like this," INNOCENCE begs.

"He will just have to wait and pray. He's in the shade, he should be okay," CLARITY sighs. "INNOCENCE, my only true friend," MARVELLOUS-ME quietly cries into the brown soil of life, feeling awfully sorry for himself.

Tick by tick, the sun slowly moves across the sky. Every ray dries the land a little more. As much as the sun gives life, it also equally takes it. Nothing is for free, and every action calls for a reaction.

A buzzard sails circles above the field in search of an afternoon snack. Only three flaps are needed to keep him gliding through the blue sky for what seems like forever. Watching him fly, INNOCENCE counts over thirty seconds until a distant patting sound smoothly travels through the silent land. The patting sound is from the warrior's wing movements, which swiftly maintain his height in the sky. As if feeling the gush of air caused by the bird, INNOCENCE closes his eyes and leans back for a moment, imagining a cool breeze stroking his face.

"One day I will fly like that!" INNOCENCE whispers into the imaginary breath of air, and starts counting again.

"The minutes are long enough, I don't need you reminding me of how slowly they actually pass," MARVELLOUS-ME cries, and hits the ground in frustration.

Soil crumbs jump into the air and as quickly as they rise, fall back down and roll to shelter. The stirred dust tickles MARVELLOUS-ME's nose and forces him to splutter once more.

"You'd better keep quiet and save your energy," CLARITY reminds him.

"You know you're not going to fly one day, don't you?" CLARITY cautiously asks INNOCENCE. "We are the home of Pimientos de Padrón; the plants that nourish their needs, so that one day they will have the essential preconditions to take on the world. We are the soul of the world's future," CLARITY proudly explains, without waiting for INNOCENCE to respond.

"Well, maybe one day, one of my peppers will fly for me," INNOCENCE shyly whispers, not letting the buzzard out of his sight.

"Yes, definitely. If that's what they want, they will have all that is needed. They will just have to set their mind to it, work hard and believe," CLARITY smiles.

In the distance, Farmer Gonzales's tractor drives up the hill. "Looks like you could get lucky, MARVELLOUS-ME," CLARITY remarks, stretching her stem to look tall.

"It's about time," MARVELLOUS-ME grumbles and presses his ear to the ground to try and detect where Farmer Gonzales is heading.

It doesn't take long, and the ground starts to tremble around them. The plants are too bushy now for the tractor to be able to make its way through the fields without harming the young leaves. So Farmer Gonzales slowly drives along the edges of the field and inspects every row with his trained eye. The closer he gets to MARVELLOUS-ME's row, the more crumbs of soil vibrate to the engine's rhythm, dancing on poor MARVELLOUS-ME's head.

"I'm here, I'm here!" MARVELLOUS-ME squeals anxiously, swallowing more dust.

"Keep calm! You'll get pneumonia if you swallow too much dust," CLARITY orders from above.

"Ha, it's alright for you up there to be saying that, isn't it! What if he misses me? By night my time could be up, if the nasty little mice and moles turn up. I'm not going to be their dinner, I can tell you that! All your talk about the world's future. Who do you think is going to do that, if I'm rubbed out?" MARVELLOUS-ME splutters, while his head bobs up and down with excitement.

"It's not as though Farmer Gonzales can hear you, MARVELLOUS-ME, King of the future," CLARITY cries out in laughter.

The tractor's engine turns off and a heavy bump indicates that Farmer Gonzales has jumped from his driver's seat.

"What's he doing?" MARVELLOUS-ME desperately asks.

"Looks like he's looking for something on the trailer," INNOCENCE explains, trying to peer past the branches of his neighbours.

"Oi, guys make space, so that my friend INNOCENCE can see what's going on!" MARVELLOUS-ME shouts down the row, but nobody reacts.

"You don't honestly think we'll endanger ourselves to see what Farmer Gonzales is doing at the trailer, do you? He's probably only digging into his sandwich for lunch," CLARITY teases.

"Well, it doesn't sound like a sandwich, CLARITY. Sounds more like he is sorting some tools," says INNOCENCE, trying to interpret the clanking noises coming from the trailer.

"You're so boring sometimes! You really need to learn to pull some legs now and then. It's fun!" adds CLARITY, rolling her eyes at INNOCENCE.

"I didn't give anything away. I promise. If Farmer Gonzales is looking for a shovel, then that's not good news for MARVELLOUS-ME," INNOCENCE eagerly defends himself.

"Ah-ha," MARVELLOUS-ME screams. "How dare you say that! You're my friend! That's evil! Nobody's digging me up, right?" MARVELLOUS-ME asks desperately, trying to look over his shoulder.

"No, no, of course not. I didn't mean it like that. I just wanted to say that I don't know what Farmer Gonzales is looking for. CLARITY put me in a corner." INNOCENCE tries to explain the situation, while CLARITY is bursting with laughter. Heavy steps coming towards them end the discussion. MARVELLOUS-ME squeezes his eyes closed and mumbles some prayer.

"Oh!" escapes from CLARITY's lips once Farmer Gonzales comes into full sight.

"What?" MARVELLOUS-ME squeaks.

"You'll like this," INNOCENCE whispers, trying to calm MARVELLOUS-ME. Farmer Gonzales bends down next to MARVELLOUS-ME and lifts him up to check his stem and leaves.

"What's happened to you, little fella?" Farmer Gonzales asks, and dabs his forehead while laying MARVELLOUS-ME down again.

Farmer Gonzales lifts his arm and, in one movement, stabs something into the ground. The soil around MARVELLOUS-ME's roots is pushed together, and one fine vein snaps apart. MARVELLOUS-ME bits on his lips in agony, trying not to cry out loud.

"You'll be okay, MARVELLOUS-ME. It'll heal," INNOCENCE quickly shouts across the lane.

"He's not killing me?" MARVELLOUS-ME whispers back in an already dying mode.

"No, he's not. You'll be fine. Just hang on," CLARITY calms him.

With a wooden hammer, Farmer Gonzales starts to force the pole deeper and deeper into the ground. Every blow shakes the ground and bumps poor MARVELLOUS-ME's head.

"There we go," Farmer Gonzales tells himself and drops the hammer to the ground. Carefully, he picks MARVELLOUS-ME up again and presses his stem along a cool metal pole. He quickly twists yarn around the stem and the pole until

MARVELLOUS-ME is totally upright again. "Now, none of that nonsense again!" Farmer Gonzales warns, picking up his hammer and walking back to his tractor.

The soil jumps to the tractor's rhythm and MARVELLOUS-ME pushes himself even more against his life-saving pole.

"You got what you always wanted. Your very own pole!" CLARITY comments.

"Hey, MARVELLOUS-ME, you're back. I'm so happy for you," INNOCENCE sings out in joy, smiling across his whole face.

"Ah, I'm so blessed. Thank you. Thank you," MARVELLOUS-ME clutches the pole and rests his head against the cool metal. His head is aching, he's exhausted, but happy to be alive and standing again.

As the sun sinks, the sprinklers come on and wash away all the dust. A home is saved and fresh hope grows across the land of the hopes and dreams of Pimientos de Padrón.

Our dream's direction 5

It didn't take long for MARVELLOUS-ME to become his old self again. His self-confidence even grew, feeling safe and supported by his new silent friend, the pole. This was much to the annoyance of his neighbours. But the nuisance doesn't stay the centre of attention for long. The ancient souls are pushing their energy to the surface. It's time to blossom. It's time to be seen. The homes of Pimientos de Padrón are ready to give birth to the tiny white flowers of the future life.

"My fingers feel like they're bursting. I can feel my pulse in every fingertip," CLARITY moans. "I wish they'd get a move on. I want to see my flowers, not just feel them pulsate," she carries on, rolling her eyes.

"You can look at mine, if you want," MARVELLOUS-ME smiles triumphantly, dangling his jewelled fingers for everyone to see. "Aren't they beautiful? Look at the three of them! And over here, you can't see it from where you stand, but I tell you, five more wonderful flowers," MARVELLOUS-ME shows off, provokingly lifting his eyebrow at CLARITY.

"You're only an early bird because you can save energy thanks to the pole holding you upright. We need to ration our strength a little better," CLARITY retorts, feeling a little irritated for not being the best in class for once.

"Well, we can't have it all, can we? But don't worry, your buds will open in the next hours. You'll be number two. Little INNOCENCE's buds are still green. No chance that he will catch you up," says MARVELLOUS-ME, sardonically strewing salt into the wound.

"I'm in no hurry. I don't mind my flowers being late. We have all the time in the world. As long as they are well, that's all that matters," INNOCENCE smiles honestly, looking up and down his arms.

"You're so not competitive! It's no fun competing with you," MARVELLOUS-ME snaps, but INNOCENCE doesn't react.

"Just ignore him. It's all fine with taking your time and such. But you know, at one point our flowers will turn into peppers, and they will need to be ripe and ready once they get picked. If they are too small or too yellow, they can end up as animal feed. You need to time it perfectly. If you're too early…," CLARITY lifts her eyebrow at MARVELLOUS-ME, who just grunts at the sidelong attack, "… or too late, your path could quickly go a different way," CLARITY explains.

"So, what's wrong with animal feed?" INNOCENCE asks.

"Nothing's wrong with it. It's absolutely necessary, some will have to make the jump. I personally wouldn't want my peppers to end up being scattered in pigs' troughs though," CLARITY goes on.

"A pig trough isn't the most elegant ending. But what about a horse's trough?" INNOCENCE goes on asking.

"Uh no, you might be tall, strong and full of energy to gallop across fields. But the majestic beauty is your ending. Who wants to be glue?" MARVELLOUS-ME blurts out.

"Glue? Why would anybody be glue? I'm talking about a proud horse," says INNOCENCE, trying to make himself clear.

"Come on, INNOCENCE, not many horses are eaten around here. You have all these horse lovers that stand in front of the slaughterhouses with banners, protesting. If you actually make it past the furious mob and end up as a piece of meat, who's going to eat you? People don't like to serve horsemeat. You don't invite friends over and offer them a juicy horse steak. It just doesn't go down well," MARVELLOUS-ME bluntly explains.

"I have no clue what you are talking about. I'm thinking about being a part of a wonderful and free horse's energy." INNOCENCE does not understand what MARVELLOUS-ME is going on about.

"Free horses? Ha, horses aren't free. They pull wagons and carry people. They are locked into a little cell at night. When their life ends, it definitely ends. That's how far you will go. Nothing more than being a good-looking pack donkey," MARVELLOUS-ME laughs.

"Hmm, I agree. It looks like the better fortune from the outside. But if you want to go the animal way, it's better to be fed to a pig, cow or chicken. In most cases, you will at least have the chance of having another hit at becoming the most advanced living being," CLARITY philosophises.

"But why take the detour. We're in the fortunate situation of only having to go through it all once. We are going straight for it," MARVELLOUS-ME confidently smiles, while blowing kisses to his flowers.

"I don't know what you mean. Going straight for what?" INNOCENCE whispers, feeling he has once again missed something.

"INNOCENCE, really! You just don't do your homework, do you? You have an ancient soul spilling over with knowledge. Why don't you use it?" CLARITY complains.

"Use it? For what?" INNOCENCE shyly asks.

"To find the meaning of life. What you are here for. Where you are going and what the options are. INNOCENCE, you need to know the best path to take," CLARITY explains.

"Yep, we know where we are going, don't we ladies? Got it all worked out. We will be big numbers one day," MARVELLOUS-ME smiles with a dreamy expression, admiring his fresh flowers.

"I know, we are home to Pimientos de Padrón, the future life. Don't animals belong to the future life?" INNOCENCE asks.

"Well, of course they do, very much so. But if you can choose, don't you want to be at the top of the food chain? One of those that walk upright and make the decisions?" CLARITY suggests.

"Mine are definitely going to be human. Successful humans. We're not going to miss any of the fun," MARVELLOUS-ME butts in.

"Everyone defines fun and success in a different way," CLARITY rolls her eyes at MARVELLOUS-ME.

"You wanted your peppers to fly, didn't you? So you have the choice. Becoming a buzzard is out of question, they don't eat Pimientos de Padrón. You could become a sparrow if your peppers are dried, crushed and then used as bird feed. But that's close to impossible. Farmer Gonzales doesn't use his crop to make bird feed. Some dried remains may get picked-up by a small bird, but don't count on that. It would cost a lot of energy and planning to end up in that way. But how about steering one of those flying machines? You know, the big ones in the sky!" CLARITY smiles.

"Aeroplanes, they are called aeroplanes, and if you do very well, and I mean really well, like my little ones, you will have a small version, called a jet, all to yourself," MARVELLOUS-ME adds knowingly. "Hey INNOCENCE, make sure some of yours become a jet pilot and you can fly mine around the world," MARVELLOUS-ME cheekily smiles.

"Aeroplanes," INNOCENCE repeats.

"No, jet is what you should memorise," MARVELLOUS-ME corrects.

"How do you know about aeroplanes?" INNOCENCE asks, desperately wanting more information about the flying machines.

"Ach, it's what I always tell you. Use your soul! Your soul knows all you need. It's been reborn so many times. It knows all about the world. It can answer any question you have.

Just reach within and you will find your answer," CLARITY explains with sparkling eyes.

"How do I do that?" INNOCENCE asks, feeling that he is going to be told off any minute.

"INNOCENCE, we have been through this. Remember finding your name. What did you have to do?" CLARITY looks at him with a serious expression.

"Ah, you mean breathe deeply and connect to my soul?" INNOCENCE cautiously asks.

"Exactly! Breathe deeply and let go of any disturbing objects that don't belong to you. You need to clear your mind to become open. I mean avoid silly things that MARVELLOUS-ME has told you. Just cut them off in your mind. You don't need those, and they don't belong to you. Imagine, for example, the jet topic as a balloon attached to your arm by a fine thread. Now imagine that you have scissor fingers and you go along your arm and cut off all of the thread and just let the balloon fly. You don't need it! Wish it well while it flies away and then concentrate on your breath again," CLARITY winks at MARVELLOUS-ME.

"Pffff, you should never let a jet go!" MARVELLOUS-ME snorts.

"Now, once you feel your mind is calm, speak out in thoughts your intention to connect with your soul. And off you go. The knowledge and the reasons for your being are all there," CLARITY knowingly smiles and stretches her arms to the sky.

"So what has your soul told you?" INNOCENCE curiously asks.

"It has told me about life and living beings out there that can do nearly limitless things. They don't just stand in the ground and produce peppers like we do. I mean, don't get me wrong, we are the home of the future Pimientos de Padrón. All doors are open for our peppers, they can become the nearly limitless living beings. That's why we are incredibly important, the world depends on us," says CLARITY, seriously underlining their purpose, and MARVELLOUS-ME approvingly nods. "Imagine, my soul told me these living beings, which they call humans, have travelled to the moon. That's an entirely different planet, far, far away from here. You know, the one that takes the sun's place at night," CLARITY tells them excitedly. Tears swell in her eyes. "One day, one of mine will have all the knowledge of such inventions and go to faraway places. With what it brings back, it will enable the world to develop," CLARITY proudly gleams. INNOCENCE's jaw drops an inch, after learning about moon travel.

"Enabling the world... I guess it needs some of you lot to spend our tax money. Mine will be enabled with what this world has to offer. Fast cars, big jets with powerful engines, houses with pools going off a cliff, so you can sit in the warm water with a cocktail in your hand and watch the sun go down. Wonderful materials that dress your skin and make you look ever so good. Box-spring beds with furry blankets and sleek black cards that you can swipe everywhere to get anything you want. Lean steaks that make your mouth water. No, not a horse steak... I am talking about tender Argentine beef," MARVELLOUS-ME dreams, while saliva bubbles gather at the corner of his lips.

"Wipe your mouth and don't be so shallow," rebukes CLARITY, waking him up. "Don't listen to him, INNO-CENCE. Listen to your soul and find your own dreams of what your peppers will do in life," CLARITY recommends.

All three go quiet for a moment and watch the sun starting to sink behind the verdant green fields. After all the talk, they long for the sprinklers to refresh their veins.

"CLARITY, look at your arm. Your flowers have just opened!" INNOCENCE excitedly observes.

"Oh, oh, all this chat and I missed the opening of my first flowers. They are beautiful! Hello there," CLARITY proudly waves her arm through the cooling air. "Perfect timing, just perfect. You'll have a night's rest before the sun rises," she sings.

INNOCENCE breathes deeply, watching the moon. "Moon travel, I like that," he whispers, but his friends are too busy admiring their flowers. He inhales two more times and imagines cutting off balloons, filled with fast cars, lean steaks, jets and furry blankets. Feeling much lighter, he inhales again and connects to his soul. There are so many answers to find, so much to explore in the land of the hopes and dreams of Pimientos de Padrón.

*****

All three homes of Pimientos de Padrón are proud plants to many dainty little white flowers. INNOCENCE's are late bloomers, but he has made it into the cycle, even though he is a dreamer. The fields are covered in little white flowers that look like fluffy snow from afar.

Farmer Gonzales is very pleased with his fields. All is going well, and they have been spared any hazards. But it's early days, and the first flowers are only just flaking to the ground. Space is needed for the peppers to grow. Their little bald, plump heads peep out with the remains of the flower, decorating their necks like collarets. Busy bees are making their way from one flower to the next to collect as much pollen as possible before the flowers drop.

"Uh, that tickles," CLARITY giggles, trying to keep calm and not wave her heavy arms all over the place.

"I don't mind the bees being here. It's all part of the game. They need us and we need them," INNOCENCE explains.

"Your soul connection is working beautifully," CLARITY smiles at him.

"Thank you CLARITY, you're a fantastic teacher. Once my peppers open their eyes, I will know how to teach them and guide their way," INNOCENCE smiles back.

"What's going on, are you two suddenly lovebirds?" MARVELLOUS-ME grunts. "By the way, did you two notice? The last petals of my flowers are just in the process of dropping. My peppers can't wait. They are ready to be heard. Our voices will have to quieten down soon, to give them the space to exchange, guys," MARVELLOUS-ME orders.

"Oh God, imagine that? Thirty MARVELLOUS-ME's or more all talking about unnecessary luxury and their "we need this and that"," pouts CLARITY.

"You're just jealous that you didn't win the race," MARVELLOUS-ME smiles, and lifts his eyebrow towards CLARITY.

But his cockiness doesn't last. A thick drop comes whistling down from the sky, splatters, and little pieces fly left and right, hitting CLARITY and INNOCENCE on the edges of their leaves.

"Ouch! What was that?" MARVELLOUS-ME shouts. "Whatever it was, keep it to yourself, next time," CLARITY shouts back, examining her speckled leaves. "You could have hit one of mine," she grumbles and turns her other arm in all directions.

"Oh dear, MARVELLOUS-ME, your pepper bud!" INNOCENCE screams.

"What? What are you squeaking about?" MARVEL-LOUS-ME asks, frantically turning his head and arms at the same time.

"Oh my God! Oh my God! I've been hit. Quickly, some-body do something. Number three is suffocating. CLARITY, INNOCENCE, do something!" MARVELLOUS-ME des-perately screams. MARVELLOUS-ME's third pepper is ab-solutely covered with white bird-poo. The weight of the mass is bending the poor pepper's branch, and an icicle formation is making its way to the ground. Every now and then, a drop forms and hits the brown soil.

"I don't know what to do, MARVELLOUS-ME," IN-NOCENCE cries, whishing he could help his friend.

"I'm really sorry, MARVELLOUS-ME, but we can't do anything. You'll have to wait for the sprinklers and hope they can wash it off," CLARITY tries to calm him.

"It's lunchtime! It'll be hours until we get water. Number three won't make it with this sun," MARVELLOUS-ME desperately shouts. CLARITY and INNOCENCE exchange a sorry expression and remain quiet.

The sun fiercely accentuates the time of day with its pitiless heat. The milky-yellow rays seem so harmless, as if they were only indicating how dusty the air is. The abstraction only takes your mind off the sun's sole purpose of innocently burning everything that is in its path. The white bird-poo perfectly reflects the sun's rays, and supports its work. It doesn't take long before the white icicle stops dripping, and a hard crust covers the tender pepper.

"Ahh, it hurts. Everything is pulling together. It's shrivelling," MARVELLOUS-ME sobs, not losing sight of his pepper number three.

The sun creeps on, there are still hours to go before it will pass the baton over to the moon. The rays of the sun play around the dried white icicle and enchant it, until it cannot stand it anymore, gives way and little cracks burst open, revealing the once protected inner self. Innocent new mass squeezes out through the cracks and offers itself as a new playground to the relentless light of day. The sun works its way perfectly, continuing to dry everything. The finest rays of heat find their ways through the finest cracks and leave no prisoners. MARVELLOUS-ME's pepper number three continuously dries and shrivels up.

"I can't feel it anymore! It's gone all numb," MARVELLOUS-ME mumbles, lost in self-pity. With widened shocked eyes, INNOCENCE blinks at CLARITY, looking for help. But there is nothing CLARITY can do but apologetically smile, before looking back to the ground in order to not have to witness the scene any further.

The hands of the sky tick on, and distant chirping from the ancient oak tree witnesses the new life of young buzzards. They will soon sail across the land like their mother, and awaken dreams of flying in others. The sound sends a rush of blood through INNOCENCE's veins, and, for a moment, the thought of birds builds excitement within him. As quick as the happy feeling awakens inside of him, just as quickly the daunting reality of what is happening to his friend kills off any need of outburst. A little embarrassed by what has overcome him, he looks away from MARVELLOUS-ME, hoping that no sudden change of colour will give him away.

The sky's bright blue colour gradually changes to a wonderful pink, followed by the most forgiving bright orange. As much harm as the sun can do, it can also project such beauty.

A clinking sound is followed by a coughing hiss and, as on every evening, fresh water sprays up from the ground and clears the air. Thousands of wet drops bounce down onto the leaves of the homes of Pimientos de Padrón. The moment they have all waited for has come - it's watering time after an emotional day in the sun.

"Ah, at last," CLARITY sighs, stretching her head to the sky and closing her eyes to enjoy the feeling of water running down her face.

"Uhhh, gentle now," MARVELLOUS-ME pleads, not letting his hit bud out of his sight. Gradually, the water pressure rises and the dust on their leaves drips to the ground. The dried icicle at first doesn't move and even seems to suck up some of the water. The growing water pressure is too much, though. The icicle sways from side to side like a seesaw, persuading the branch to give way. The green finger thins, and before MARVELLOUS-ME can shout out one more time, it rips and pulls a fine thread, leaving it dangling just an inch from the ground. Shocked to death by the sight, INNOCENCE turns pale.

"Let it go, MARVELLOUS-ME! Let it go before it does more damage," CLARITY orders. Biting his lip, MARVELLOUS-ME squeezes his eyes closed. There's a dull thud and MARVELLOUS-ME's hit arm springs up in the air, nervously shivers and comes back into its original position before the hit. But there is no bald, little pepper on the end anymore. Instead a brown stub reaches to the sky.

"Number three, number three has gone,"MARVELLOUS-ME cries in shock.

"I am really sorry, MARVELLOUS-ME,"INNOCENCE mumbles, feeling terrible.

The innocence of their being has been destroyed by a common happening. Life has shown itself from its hard side for the first time. Bad karma has struck, and the sorrow of loss is a new feeling. The first Pimiento de Padrón did not make its way. It couldn't even grow to its full size before falling.

Or is this part of the plan?

Is there a reason behind what we call unfortunate failure?

In the view of the homes of Pimientos de Padrón, this pepper is taking a detour. Maybe the pepper's seeds are developed and a new home can grow. But the timing would be bad, and the new plant could never catch-up before the snow falls. The pepper's flesh could become food for a field mouse or insect. Or, the most likely version, the remains will turn into prosperous ground for souls to be reborn and develop. This would mean that pepper number three played an important role in securing the hopes and dreams of future generations to come.

But in the moment of sorrow and loss, it is difficult to see the meaning. Maybe the true reason will never show, and the chain of events will never be blessed. They will only be stamped on memories as an unfortunate happening.

*****

The event of losing a pepper doesn't go down well and is the ingredient of rumours all over the fields. The sky above has suddenly become dangerous, and this common occurrence is blown-up into a tragic, life-threatening event.

Even though hit by the loss, the attention is welcomed by MARVELLOUS-ME. He has become known overnight, and is included in his neighbours' prayers. He has experienced real life's tragedy. Not just uploaded information from his soul, but real, heart-ripping sadness, experienced on his own body. His input, thought and knowledge are looked for and valued.

As the peppers grow, the time comes for the homes of Pimientos de Padrón to draw back and allow the platform for the peppers' hopes and dreams to develop.

CLARITY is proud that hers are growing perfectly, and it's her pleasure to lean back and watch them.

INNOCENCE is his dreamy self, and though his peppers are a little smaller than the average, he doesn't miss a second of listening in to their growth and sending them thoughts of air machines, the freedom of flight and peace. From his point of view, their little bodies are a perfect fit for a cockpit to explore the world by air.

MARVELLOUS-ME, well, MARVELLOUS-ME's peppers are plump and round. Their juicy bodies are fit for a comfortable life in a likewise plum surrounding.

At the point where their branches meet, the three different characters find a platform to discuss and exchange. A circle of totally different peppers hang together and share their dreams.

On CLARITY's branch, Marple and Winston lead the field of knowledge and bright thought.

Apollo and Clark carry forward INNOCENCE's dreams of flight and free spirit, while Kim and Flavio weave a life of luxury on MARVELLOUS-ME's side.

It's only a matter of hours before the peppers develop speech and the area turns into a chit-chat coffee room. As the sun goes down, the fields enjoy a final night of silence in the land of the hopes and dream of Pimientos de Padrón. In the days to come, nothing will be the same anymore. The prosperous land has produced its future generation, and they are on the threshold of awakening.

A destination of choice 6

As the sun rises the next day, the land holds its breath in anticipation of who will be the first to speak. The dreams of the Pimientos de Padrón showcase the future lives awaiting them, and being able to listen to them talk is the short harvesting moment of their supporting plants. The homes of Pimientos de Padrón all know that they did well, and that their efforts were not in vain.

The first sunbeams tickle the faces of MARVELLOUS-ME's peppers. Flavio rubs the sleep from his eyes and peers into the bushy arms of his surroundings.

"One, two. Oh, and another two little ones over there," he says, counting his neighbours. Looking up to his carrying branch, he detects another plump-looking pepper. Its coat is wonderfully green and looks freshly polished. He likes the sight. Hanging on the same stem can only mean that he is just as perfect.

"Yes!" he congratulates himself and strokes the side of his tummy. "Wonderful me! Wonderful us," he sings up to his siblings.

"Uff, what's this noise about? I know I'm wonderful. There's no need to shout so early in the morning," Kim complains, while carefully combing her lashes. "Of course we are wonderful. I mean, look at us!" she chimes in an elegant voice.

"Don't worry, Kim. You've had enough sleep. Too much will only swell your eyes," Flavio snaps, picking up the reason for her complaint.

Their home, MARVELLOUS-ME, smiles to himself. His peppers have grown quicker than he thought. They are automatically using his soul knowledge, no introduction needed.

"How much sleep is appropriate in your point of view, Flavio?" a voice asks from CLARITY's home. For a second all goes quiet.

"Hmm, you must be... Marple, right?" Flavio asks.

"Precisely, I am. It took you a while!" Marple smirks at him.

"That's only because you and your sibling Winston hang so close. It's difficult to tell you apart. Are you twins?" asks Flavio, pretending to be curious.

"Exactly, we are. We are nourished by the same soul," Marple nods.

"Obviously!" replies Flavio. "As you are so polite, let me introduce ourselves to you. I am Flavio, as you know. And over here is my beautiful sibling, Kim."

"There are more of us on the other side, but that's another arrondissement," Kim smiles.

"Arrondissement? Is this Paris?" Winston cannot help but ask.

"No, obviously not," retorts Kim, "This is the land of the hopes and dreams of Pimientos de Padrón. We are the peppers of the future and my music will play in Paris. The city of chic, dance and fashion," says Kim, smoothing her eyebrows.

"The city of love," a dreamy voice whispers. All four look in the direction of the whispered voice. Apollo stretches himself and yawns, wraps his arms around himself and tilts his head to one side. With a happy smile on his face, he lets himself wander back into his dream world.

"That must be INNOCENCE's lot," Marple comments, studying the two sleeping peppers.

"So, you were saying, Flavio, how much sleep do you think is needed before your eyes swell?" asks Marple, reanimating their discussion.

"I live according to the 1.5 hour sleep rule. My soul and I have studied the sleep pattern, and I can tell you, it takes 1.5 hours for one full sleep cycle to go from light to deep sleep and back again. To be your best, you should always awaken when you are in a light sleep phase. You will reach this phase every 1.5 hours after you have gone to sleep. So after 1.5, 3, 4.5, 6, 7.5 hours and so on … 1.5 hours of sleep is too little. Around 8 hours a night is recommended, so you should go with 9 hours, or maybe 7.5 if you are fit. Personally I think going more than 9 hours can make you look blotchy. Look at INNOCENCE's lot to know what I mean," Flavio smiles with an evil look.

"Don't be so nasty, Flavio. INNOCENCE's peppers are all males," Kim nudges him.

"What are you saying? We guys don't need to look fresh? Blotchy eyes are okay for us, are they?" Flavio grunts at her.

"You know what I mean," stabs Kim, turning to comb her hair.

"So Paris. Why the French capital?" continues Marple, changing the subject.

"As I said, I'm striving for a life of beauty and meaning. One day, I will change the way humans dress, without forgetting history and the compulsory sprinkle of chic. Paris is where that's done today, and that's exactly where I'm going," Kim proudly explains, and mimics an elegant walk with her arm.

"But is what we wear so important? In my view it's about what we do," Winston chimes in. "I will lead in whatever I wear," he concludes with a smile.

"So what are you thinking of leading? Your household? A building project? A town or even a country?" asks Kim, not feeling the least offended.

"I will start off small and then grow," replies Winston, "One day I'm sure to lead at least a country."

"Well then, while you're growing, be sure to stay in contact with me. Once you're big, I'll give you a hand, dress-wise, to make it to the really, really large stage. Clothes make the man, you know," Kim offers with a sweet smile.

"I will remember and give you a ring," Winston winks back.

"Will you make flying machine suits?" a shy voice whispers, making all the peppers turn in one direction.

"Apollo?" Kim asks, after a short pause.

"Yes, it's me. I'll need a flying machine suit, made of thin but warm material. Slightly slippery, so I can easily slide into the small seat of my rocket machine," Apollo dreams on.

"Not sure that's my genre," says Kim, tightly pulling her eyebrows together, while Apollo just looks at her puzzled.

"She means, it's probably not her cup of tea. Not the sort of thing she does," says Marple, clearing the question marks.

"Oh, okay. Well, I guess NASA already has what I need," Apollo shyly smiles.

"NASA who?" Flavio asks.

"The National Aeronautics and Space Administration. It's the agency for aerospace research," Apollo proudly explains.

"Is that in Paris too?" Flavio asks.

"No, it's in the United States of America. Cape Canaveral, Florida, is the base I will be at," Apollo beams. "But aren't we all going to Paris?" Flavio can't give up.

"Why would we all going to Paris?" INNOCENCE's second pepper, Clark, joins the discussion.

"Cause Kim said so," answers Flavio, making his point.

"So far, only Kim is going to Paris. That doesn't mean we all have to," adds Apollo, defending his dream.

"But isn't it going to be difficult for the pickers to put us all in the right country box? How will they know?" Clark continues with his thread of questions.

"That's a good point," Flavio adds.

"They'll just know, it's written all over our faces and anyway, that's not our problem. They will have to work it out," Kim smiles.

"But your face is really covered. How will they know what's beneath all that colour?" Clark asks, without realising what he actually just said.

"You watch it over there," Kim snarls. "What's wrong with some colour to underline where I'm going? The theatres of Paris are full of masks. If you want to make it big in the scene, you've got to start practicing young," Kim explains, pinning him with her dark eyes.

"You are drifting off! Calm down over there," Marple tries to get the conversation back to the subject.

"Mesdames, Messieurs, this is the Paris line. Get friendly with it, that's where we are going," Kim chuckles.

"Because you want to be chic, we all have to go to Paris?" Winston barks. "Monsieur, Monsieur, excuse-moi!" Kim tickles on.

"You watch it, or I'll make sure you land in a Marseille banlieue," Winston spits.

"Uh, oh," Kim smiles.

"Calm down, Winston. She's only winding you up. Let me work this out," says Marple, soothing him, and looking up and down the row in a knowing way. "So let's get this straight. Over there on MARVELLOUS-ME's branch we have Kim, who's using too much make-up because she is preparing for chic Paris. And at the back there's Flavio. Thinking about your name leads me in direction of Italy, right?" Marple analyses.

"Ha, I definitely am, the further south the better. I see myself at the head of a long table. Everyone listening to me, and then I do it. I take the decision everyone is waiting for. Nobody will question me, I am the clan's Don," Flavio dreams.

"That's enough, I get it. You're going to Italy to become a mafia icon," snaps Marple, shutting him up. "Okay, Paris and Italy," she continues, "Over to INNOCENCE's lot. We have Apollo living his aerospace dreams in Florida. And Clark?" asks Marple, trying to put him on the spot.

"I don't know," Clark mumbles. "I'd just like to be happy, with a lot of nature around me," he says, looking down at the brown soil.

"One easy one." Marple smiles. "Now, to us, CLARITY's peppers. Winston, where's your dream taking you?" Marple asks her sibling.

"I'm going to lead a country. It's definitely going to be an ancient place with history. I'm a little back and forth, maybe somewhere in the Orient," Winston wonders in a royal tone. Marple's eyes thin down to a line.

"Can we please stay with Europe? It will make things easier. There are many places with history for you to lead," she commands.

"Hmm, then maybe I'll go to Italy and arrest Flavio," Winston chuckles.

"Don't get your hopes high, my clan will be on to you," Flavio warns, wagging his index finger.

"Shush, I'm solving our case," Marple interrupts the gamecocks. "Now, I see myself at MI6, that means London," Marple sparkles. "That leaves us with one for the US, four for Europe and one that hasn't made his mind up, but would surely find his place of peace in one of the European countries. Apollo, I'm really sorry, but you should think about new destinations closer to ours. Our destination is set for good old Europe," Marple smiles, feeling pleased with herself.

"You'll do fine in France. We have airspace," Kim winks.

"Don't let her put you under pressure. London is a grand spot for all sorts of air travel," interrupts Marple, trying to overbid Kim. Apollo is confused and looks close to tears, seeing his dream vanishing down the drain.

"Don't worry, Apollo. Start off in London, and then, when you're ready, fly across the Atlantic and make it big time in the US," Marple smiles kindly.

The talk about the chosen destination carries on. Not even the vibrant colours of the sun, mixing with the rising night, can distract them. Much is still to be thought about and discussed before the picking season starts. Hopes are to be shared and challenged. While a few are certain of their future, others need help and inspiration.

Only the overpowering rustling noise of the sprinklers forces peace. The peppers close their eyes and enjoy their daily wash. Their wet, glittering bodies can be seen from afar and reflect the golden colours of dancing fireflies. An owl hoots from the tree, while the dark night sky settles in the land of the hopes and dreams of Pimientos de Padrón. Ideas of their future destinations spark dreams and animate their imaginations of the life to come.

*****

After a peaceful night, the sun gets up early and warms the pepper's bodies. Another warm day is expected, with lots of time for further discussions.

Most of the peppers in the European line are up as soon as the yellow rays touch their growing curves. Clark, on INNOCENCE's stem, has had a hard night. He understands that the destination of their line has been chosen, but he cannot quite get his head around why. What's the reason for the commotion? Questions about questions are burning in his mind. He can't wait to ask and learn more. At the same time though, a wave of worry floats through him. What if everyone understands except himself?

But he can't hold back, there's too much he must be able to figure out. Where is he going? And will yesterday's decisions work in his favour?

"Marple?" he whispers over to CLARITY's branch, hoping to find some time with her alone before all the others get chatty.

"Hmm, Clark. What are you doing up at this early hour? I thought you guys don't open your eyes before lunchtime." Marple rubs her face.

"I couldn't sleep. I have some questions I have to ask," Clark whispers on.

"So go on, ask," encourages Marple.

"Okay, so we're going to good old Europe, right? But why does that matter?" asks Clark.

"Well, that's what we worked out. It's the place where the majority of us can fulfil our dreams," Marple doesn't understand his question. "Yes, but how are we going to fulfil those dreams. We are peppers!" Clark continues.

"So? What's wrong with being a pepper?" asks Kim, joining the discussion. "Nothings wrong with it," Clark mumbles, feeling caught. His worry about looking silly is already turning into reality, and he hasn't even asked a fraction of what's on his mind.

"Well then. What are the questions about? Feel proud to be born as the future generation. Hold your head up high and cheer to the next day." Kim demonstrates what she means and stretches herself towards the sun.

"But... Marple, why are we the future generation?" Clark whispers over to Marple.

But Winston cannot hold back his words, and he jumps in. "Humans eat. Humans are constantly hungry and they love us peppers. We are something they can't get enough of, and they eat us in large amounts without noticing. Believe me, my soul has told me all about it," he explains.

"So, these humans are going to eat us?" Clark asks hesitantly. He doesn't feel sure whether he should like the direction this is going.

"Yes, they will. Me, most probably, first," Winston self-consciously smiles.

"Don't be daft. You're skinny and long. We two over here are plump and perfectly shaped. We'll be first down," Kim butts in.

"I hope not, you could put them off taking another one. You're a hot chick. I can see it from the way your red tail mixes into the green," Winston complains.

"That will go away. Just give me a few more days in the sun, and I'll grow a perfect camouflage," Kim proudly gives back.

"Anyway, our long bodies will show up. We will stick out in every crowd," Winston puts his point.

"Will it hurt when they eat us?" Clark asks worriedly.

"It's not going to be a nice moment. But the real pain's before, when they fry us," Flavio whispers into the round. "And then they sprinkle salt on our fresh wounds," he carries on with large eyes, and the small crowd gasps. "After all of that, you won't actually feel too much by the time they eat you," Flavio finishes.

"That's enough for me, I'm just going to fall from the branch and sacrifice myself to the next generation," Clark squeals.

"Don't be silly. You have the chance to become the future, and all you want to do with it is drop from the branch?" Flavio exclaims in disgust.

"Some of us have to stay back. If Clark offers himself, let him," Kim oozes.

"Yes, I'm truly thinking of falling from the branch. Sounds much more natural than being fried, salted and then chewed to death. I don't see the point," says Clark, shaking his head.

"You obviously don't understand the point," says Marple, wrinkling her eyebrows. "

No, I don't. Why should I travel to old Europe to be tortured and eaten?" asks Clark, raising his voice.

"Cos you want to be the next generation!" barks Marple. Clark looks over at her, feeling totally puzzled. Nothing is making sense, and he starts to wonder whether he is missing an important piece.

"Clark, look. If you are lucky enough that a human of your choice picks you and actually eats you, you will blend into its body and become human," explains Marple, excitedly trying to clear the situation.

"But we are like, really small. How could we take over such a large body?" Clark asks.

"We are small but very effective, and extremely powerful. Don't let the fact of our size worry you. If we were large, they couldn't eat us," Flavio explains with a knowing look.

"What about all the other things they eat?" Clark needs to know.

"Other things, tssst. As you say, these are other things, with other names and other dreams. They have nothing to do with our world. No one knows what they want, so that's not our problem." Kim makes her point, and all nod. The fact that they have other dreams makes sense to Clark, and he feels a little more at ease.

In his mind, he goes through the situation to be sure he has worked it all out.

After being picked, I will go off to good old Europe, be bought by a human of my choice, fried, salted and chewed. I won't like that moment, but it's necessary for the further process to take part. Then I blend with the human and become that person. That's it, he thinks.

"But how do I make sure a human of my choice chooses me?" he blurts out, quite to his surprise. There's a moment of silence, and some of the peppers pretend to be studying their branches.

"Because you will think very, very hard of the human you want to be, and believe, believe and believe again. Our thoughts attract matching humans. So don't you dare think of my human, and I would very much advise you to not to think of Flavio's. Make sure you stay with your own dream. Repeat it inwardly, every moment of your life, and your deepest wish will come true. You'll see. You alone shape your future with your own strong will," Marple advises.

Repeat, repeat. Believe, believe," all the peppers loudly memorise. Then there is silence, while they all reflect on what has been spoken.

Each pepper knows that it must spend more time with its dream to be sure of its direction. Many ideas and fantasies must be examined from all sides. Examined and experimented, tested and analysed. No stone can be left unturned. It is too vital to miss their one-time shot at realising their dream and becoming the future generation. Making their souls proud of their hard work and their dedication by becoming their higher meaning of being.

Once again, night falls and fireflies dance in the moonlight. Dreams are dreamt and hopes are fed in the land of the hopes and dreams of Pimientos de Padrón.

Our view
on fate **7**

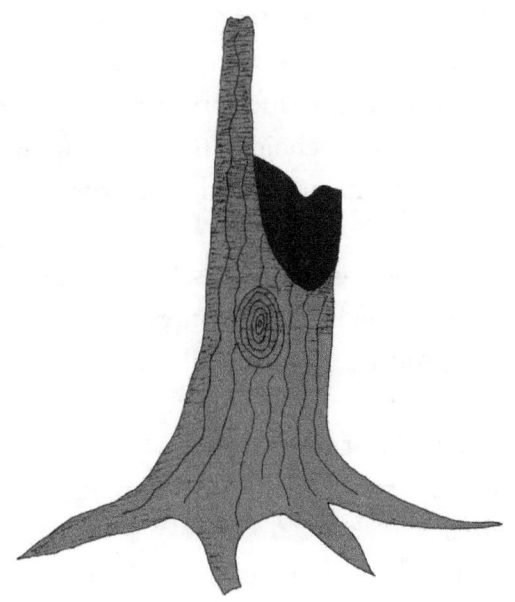

"Marple, why the humans?" Clark whispers the following afternoon.

It's past lunchtime, the sun is still high in the sky, but the air is thicker than usual. The heat and humidity are taking their toll, and little wet drops are forming on the peppers' bodies.

"What do you mean, Clark?" Marple sighs, trying to wriggle some of the tickling drops from her side.

"I mean, why don't we target some other living beings? Why just humans?" Clark innocently expands his question.

"They are the leading life form on this planet. No other living being has more choices than the humans," explains Marple with a slight undertone of confusion about the question.

"Humans can fly air machines," Apollo marvels.

"They design their own clothes and present them to others on long runways," Kim smiles.

"They lead and take dangerous decisions," Flavio whispers in a "you know what I mean" tone.

"And some arrest others for making those choices," Winston grins.

"Pfff, that's if you can catch me. You'll never find me," Flavio snorts back. "That won't be hard, I'll follow the pasta trail all the way south till I've got ya," Winston chuckles, quite enjoying himself and making Flavio snort one more time.

"We're actually very lucky, not many other living beings like to eat us. It's more a coincidence if one does, or a life-threatening situation of hunger is forcing them to," Marple adds.

"I call that faith or good karma. We're supposed to take over the humans. We've done it for years and have led the world to a better place," Kim sighs. The sky grumbles above them.

"Looks like someone up there doesn't agree," Marple remarks.

"That was a grumble of approval," Kim returns sharply. But the peppers are not really convinced.

The sky is quickly turning grey, and the wind is picking up. The sun suddenly vanishes behind a dark cloud.

"What's going on?" Apollo wonders.

"Uhh, I like this wind. It's drying my make-up, and it's practice for when I stand in the spotlight. I can already see the fans blowing my hair back in a Charlie's Angel style for the cameras," Kim sighs.

"Keep your head down girl, I am not sure this is that kind of situation," Marple warns, licking her finger and holding it up in the air. "The wind is picking-up from the west, and the air temperature is dropping dramatically. I recommend getting under a leaf if you can, and hold on for your life," Marple orders sharply.

"Are you sure?" Winston asks, feeling a little worried, knowing that detective Marple is rarely wrong.

Lightning flashes across the sky and the clouds grumble terribly, overpowering any other sound.

"I'm sure! Get under that leaf of yours!" Marple shouts to her brother.

Down on the ground, some leaves gather, jump into the air and play with the wind. Their faint rustling isn't heard for long. Another arrow of lightning brightens the sky and, unforgivingly, hits the old oak tree in the middle of the field. The tree's bark cracks and springs apart, releasing the frightening sound of ancient life squealing. The dry wood sparks like fireworks, followed by a ruthless, bright flame. It only takes seconds before the old tree is burning like a giant match. In shock, the peppers scream and cover their ears with their hands so as not to have to witness the oak's desperate fight for life.

"Water, we need water. The fire will spread if we don't get help," Marple shouts in desperation. "Guys, concentrate. We all need to concentrate on water. All of our hopes put together can save us," she orders, looking around with a serious expression. "Don't close your eyes in fear, close your eyes in hope, and pray," she pleads, closing her eyes and going into meditation. Winston immediately follows his sister. Kim hesitates, and looks to Flavio for advice.

"We're going to burn!" Flavio blurts out, watching the flames' greedy hands reach for the homes of Pimientos de Padrón near to the tree.

Suffocating smoke stalks down the lanes and plays around the feet of the peppers. Giggling every time, it puffs itself up and rises an inch.

"Calm down, Flavio, concentrate! Concentrate on life and the water we need to save us," echoes Marple's voice through the smoke. Apollo and Clark squint their eyes and bury their heads in their arms. The sky above them thunders and the ground trembles under the force.

A tractor's engine starts up in the distance. Hope rises; Farmer Gonzales is on his way.

The sky darkens further with thick, bulging clouds. A wave of cold air sweeps through the smoke, and there they are - the first longed-for pearls from heaven. The clouds have opened, and thick drops of rain shoot down to earth and bounce off their home's leaves.

"It's raining!" Kim squeals. "Paris is safe," she sings and holds her hands up to the sky.

Her excitement is killed by an awful cracking sound, coming from the oak tree. One large branch has given up its fight and is hanging by only a thread. A second later, a thud and rising dust sign the branch's death sentence. The homes of the Pimientos de Padrón beneath the branch are buried.

The ruthless flames fight against the rain for more territory, while the ground beneath the peppers starts to bounce to the rhythm of Farmer Gonzales's tractor. The peppers know it's now a fight between Farmer Gonzales, the rain and their opponent, the hungry flames. As the sky grumbles once more, the rain shower thickens, and gushes of water flood the fields. The sprinklers go on and the battle for survival is fought from all sides. The flames hiss and growl as they are beaten to the ground. Their long orange fingers try to grasp another thin branch and continue their being. Like a volcano, the heat's centre spits red, sending burning spears up into the air that fly across the fields. But the cold water has the final say today, and forces the flames to retreat.

The oak tree and the surrounding homes of Pimientos de Padrón sizzle as the heat dies down, and the enemy closes his red eyes in defeat. Cold smoke rises to the sky, marking the battlefield for miles around.

The heavy rain continues to fall on the fields, and drowns the earth. The dust from the fire sprinkles the peppers' bodies as a final word of warning, marking its power.

Totally soaked, but relieved, the peppers one by one open their eyes.

"Is everyone okay?" Marple asks, checking her dripping wet body. The heavy rain makes it difficult to understand each other.

"I'm here," Winston shouts back.

"I'm good, but Flavio is having difficulties protecting himself fully under just one leaf," Kim screeches, not making Flavio feel any more comfortable, but, at this moment, nobody cares.

On INNOCENCE's branch, the remains of smoke float to the sky.

"Apollo? Clark? Are you okay?" Marple shouts, trying to overpower the rain with her dominant voice.

"Something smells a bit burnt," Kim rubs her nose.

"This has nothing to do with dreams, it smells really strange," Apollo says, shivering in a weak voice.

"Where is Clark?" Marple asks, trying not to sound worried.

"Oh, Clark!" Apollo screams, seeing his brother dangling by only a few threads.

"I am still here, guys. I just wonder for how long," Clark tries to calm them down with a weak voice. "One of these fire spears came right for me," he explains.

"Hang on my friend, hopefully the rain won't last too long," Winston shouts.

"How badly are you hit? Do you feel you're still burning?" asks Marple, trying to clarify the situation. "Apollo, have a look, will you!" she commands.

"I don't really think I want to see it," he cries, pulling his protecting leaf closer.

"Come on, it's your brother, for God's sake!" yells Winston.

"His holding stem has gone all brown with some black parts. It looks like coal. But no flames, I think the fire is gone," Apollo whispers from beneath his leaf. "But he is unprotected now, he is dangling too far from the leaves," he adds in a scared tone.

Above them, it sounds as if the clouds are bumping together, releasing even more rain. Large drops fly past them and jump up from the puddles before becoming part of a rising stream. The sound deafens any further words. Each pepper is now on his or her own. Nature is striking down at them with all its power. The water has saved them from the flames, but who will hold back the rain?

A night of fear and cold awaits the future generation. Only exhaustion will lull them into a wakeful sleep. Tonight, hopes of survival and protection grow in the land of the hopes and dreams of Pimientos de Padrón. Fear of not being able to make their longed-for destination takes over their innocent minds.

*****

After a long, dark and wet night, the rising sun dries the earth's tears. The peppers sparkle in the early morning sun-light, and light up the fields in a forgiving colour. Only the old oak tree is burnt to cinders, and the surrounding black soil stands as a memorial of what has happened. A smell of burnt wood and wet soil wafts through the lanes.

"I think we were really lucky. I mean, look at us…," Kim's voice suddenly dies down, remembering that one of them is still hanging on to his life.

Clark's injury takes its toll. He is not sufficiently fed to meet the need to reach his final size. This would no longer be threatening for some pepper families, but, in the case of INNOCENCE's peppers, every extra day of growth is absolutely needed. They are small peppers, who were born a little late.

"Kim, really!" Winston grunts at her.

"No worries, Winston. I'm still here. Sticks and stones may break my bones, but words will never hurt me," Clark giggles. Dangerously, he starts to sway.

"Stay still! You only have two threads left. You don't want to giggle them away," Marple orders. "Looks like the rain has softened your broken branch," she analyses.

"Oh, Clark, I'm so afraid. What if you drop," Apollo cries.

"Don't worry, Apollo. My destiny will choose the right path to take. I have full basic trust in life," Clark smiles.

"Shush!" Marple orders.

"Can you hear that too?" Winston suddenly asks.

"Yes, that's Farmer Gonzales's tractor. There is some cleaning-up to be done. I mean, look at our poor old oak tree," Marple remarks.

"If I was Farmer Gonzales, I would snap your head off, Clark. You're pointlessly using up soul energy. It won't hurt - a quick break of the neck is the best way to do it," Flavio bluntly recommends.

"You're terrible, my brother," Kim snorts, feeling quite amused.

"Oh shut up, how dare you!" glares Winston. "And anyway, you've missed the point, you dummy! If Clark is picked early, he would still live on, that's not a death sentence. We will all be picked, earlier or later," Winston adds, educating him.

"Yeah, smarty pants, but still, he wouldn't be eaten," Flavio return.

"Why not? We're close to our required size," Marple challenges.

"Cause I say so. He'll be put in a mixer and used as chicken food. If Farmer Gonzales or the mixer doesn't break his neck, then the chicken's beak will stab him to death. He will then mould to a hen. I will find you and serve you as my Christmas roast," Flavio boasts.

"Ha, ha," Marple cries out. "That means dear Clark will take you over after you have filled your tummy. That will be the end of the Italian mafia," says Marple, enjoying herself.

"You two CLARITY peppers have just made it to the top of my neck-breaking list. Watch it!" says Flavio, pinning them with an evil look.

The peppers' laughter dies down with the sound of squeaking brakes. But this time it's not just one pair of heavy boots that lands on the ground. Farmer Gonzales is not alone. After some talking, the small crowd breaks up in different directions.

"What's going on," Apollo whispers.

"I'm not sure," Marple rubs her chin and stretches her neck.

Two strong men inspect the old oak tree and unpack some dangerous looking tools. A cord is pulled, and a nasty sawing noise fills the area.

"What's that? It hurts my ears," Apollo complains.

"I guess it's time to say goodbye to the old oak tree," Winston remarks, watching the two men get close to the tree's stem.

It's a sad sight for all the peppers, even for Flavio. The old oak tree has been the centre of the field for centuries. As the saw scratches the dead bark's surface, a terrible screeching sound pierces marrow and bone. The ground beneath the peppers trembles through the force.

"Oh, oh," Clark bounces. "This isn't good," he squeals. Like an exhausted bedspring, his second thread jumps from his head and leaves the peppers gasping.

"This isn't looking good at all," Kim remarks. Footsteps are coming towards them, leaving no time for further discussions. Each plant is efficiently checked and dead or harmed leaves removed. The humans work quickly without losing any time in analysis. Their hands comb through each bush and take away whatever is not firmly attached. With widened eyes, the peppers watch what's happening. They are next.

Coarse hands brush through their homes. Yellow and brown leaves are taken away. Within only a split second, Clark is found, and snapped off his branch.

"Clark!" Apollo screams, seeing him fly through the air towards a wicker basket.

"Don't worry my friends! I'll stay behind and secure the next generation. I'm not sad, this is my dream of nature being fulfilled," is all Clark manages before he vanishes into the moving basket.

Shocked by the sudden event, the peppers hang in silence. Not even the crumbling of the oak's timber can shake them out of their thoughts. Life quickly changes, and takes unexpected turns. The day before they were all happy, teasing each other and shaping their dreams. Then the night's events, nature striking and one of them left injured, but alive. And now a decision has been taken without discussion or questioning. One of them has been sacrificed to the next generation of souls and peppers.

"Marple, do you really think Clark dreamt of staying behind?" Apollo whispers.

"I don't know. He must have. There's no other way to explain what has just happened. I mean, he did mention that he wanted to stay in a natural surrounding. Now his dream has come true," says Marple, working out the events in her mind.

"One of us has to stay behind, that's the way things go. We should be glad and celebrate that it's done with," says Flavio, trying to cheer up his neighbours.

But his invitation isn't really well received. It feels strange to celebrate losing a friend.

"Flavio, what a blunt way of putting it," says Marple, shaking her head at him after a short silence. "But thinking about it, you're right. We should celebrate. Not because it's been done. We should clink our glasses because Clark's dream has already been fulfilled. He's a step ahead of us. We should wish him well and hope that the path in front of him is merciful," analyses Marple.

Apollo smiles for the first time this day. Clark, the pepper of INNOCENCE, did not live in vain. He actually did what he was meant to do. All is well, Apollo thinks to himself, taking a deep breath. He can feel his spirit lifting again.

"Put it any way you want, if we're having a party, I'm in on it," snorts Flavio.

"You can save the party for your future life, but we should definitely cheer," Winston smiles.

The peppers sway in synchrony, watching the sunset. Fireflies decorate their branches like little lamps. All is good, all is well. A dream has been fulfilled and has left five others behind, waiting for their path of destiny to go on, in the land of the hopes and dreams of Pimientos de Padrón.

Our shining 8

Two days later, the peppers are woken up by lots of noise coming from the edges of the fields.

"What's going on?" Flavio complains.

"The sun isn't even up properly yet," Winston agrees, rubbing his eyes.

"Ha, guys. It's the pickers!" Marple gasps, stretching her neck. Immediately all are awake.

"The pickers? Are you sure? Am I ready?" Kim nervously pats down her body. "Winston, can you still see some red patches?" she screeches. "Imagine if the humans can tell that I'm a hot one. It could prevent them from eating me," she nervously continues.

"You look fine, as always," Winston winks.

"No! I know I look fine, but what about the red patches?" Kim complains.

"You won't be presented and eaten today. We still have the travel in front of us, you know," Marple tries to shut her up. "Our final colour will develop by the time we reach our destination. If they waited until we were deep green, we would be shrivelled up by the time we arrived," Marple adds, rolling her eyes at her, making Kim stamp her foot in the air.

"Calm down, lovely. You look fine. We are the branch of MARVELLOUS-ME, remember! We will always look fantastic," Flavio calms her with a self-assured look.

Straw hats and colourful headscarves scatter across the fields and quickly move from one lane to the other. Now and then they empty their cotton bags into large wooden crates that are standing on a trailer.

"Am I big enough?" Apollo shyly asks his friends. "I think you're quite tiny," Flavio grins.

"Don't worry, some like it small. Not everyone fancies a mouthful like MARVELLOUS-ME, Flavio," Marple smiles sincerely and then turns to Flavio with a "you watch it" expression.

Apollo smiles at Marple. He likes her. She always knows what's really going on, and encourages him.

"Marple, what's going to happen now?" Apollo asks, with a worried voice.

"Our journey will begin. We will be picked and sent off to good old Europe," Marple beams.

"Will it hurt?" Apollo wants to know.

"Uh, it's like getting your hair ripped out," Flavio grins mischievously.

"God, I hope I'm not in your box," Marple sighs. "Don't listen to him, Apollo, he is just trying to scare you. You won't feel a thing," she calms him.

"I'm going to be in your box, Marple," Apollo determines.

"Good choice! INNOCENCE and CLARITY is always a good mix," Winston approves.

"A pinch of marvelousness never hurts," Kim purrs. "Let's just stay together," she suggests, with the sweetest smile.

"Is MARVELLOUS-ME's branch getting nervous?" tickles Winston.

"What's the point of breaking-up? We know each other. Everything is settled. I don't see why we should mix with others. Who knows who you might suddenly get next to you," Kim blinks.

"Can't get any worse than having a would-be mafia boss next to you," Winston remarks.

"Ha, you four will be glad to have a Padre watching over you. I will protect our clan," Flavio proudly demonstrates by waving his hand, signalling a giant hug.

As the pickers get close to the European line, the peppers can hear them singing happily. A red headscarf bobs up and down the lane next to them, whistling a tune.

"Okay, we should get ready, we will be next," Marple whispers. "Everyone, make sure you look your best. None of us wants to be mistaken for a leaf. Apollo, stretch that body of yours!" Marple commands.

"Tut, as if anybody could get me mixed-up with a plain leaf," Flavio spits back, and roles his eyes.

He would never admit it, but seeing the red headscarf coming closer also makes his nerves spin. Secretly, he arranges himself in his best pose.

"Here she comes, it's a lady," Winston comments on the scene.

"She hasn't emptied her bag. Hopefully she has enough space for all of us. Otherwise we could get split up before we reach the trailer," Marple says, becoming jittery.

"I will tell her to just leave Flavio out, that will make a lot of space," Winston laughs.

The picker changes her whistling to a merry song. Her voice is beautiful, and hypnotises the peppers. Flavio has no choice but to hang with his mouth open.

"Look at him! I wouldn't be surprised if he suddenly trades his profession to be closer to her," Marple giggles.

"Oh, oh," Apollo cries. He's the first to be picked. A small hand comes down towards him. For a second he can see the lady's face. She is young and pretty, but something dazzles his eyes and he is blinded for a second. Then he realizes. She is carrying a little, silver knife in her hand that is reflecting the sunlight. Scared stiff, Apollo closes his eyes and bites his teeth together. He feels his body lifted up into the air, quickly turned and then laid against a soft material.

"Wow!" Winston and Marple shout as they are placed next to him. The picker pulls her cotton bag straight and the three peppers slide down the canvas, bumping into other Pimientos de Padrón at the bottom. It's dark and gloomy inside the cotton bag. The air is thick and dry.

"Wow, that was fun," Winston squeals. "I wouldn't mind sliding down there again," he giggles in anticipation.

"Are you okay, Apollo?" Marple caringly asks.

"Yes, I am okay. Stay with me, won't you?" Apollo whispers through the darkness.

The picker's bag is opened again. Sunlight shines through the opening and blinds the peppers. A small fist shoots into the bag, releasing more peppers.

"Yeeh-heee!" Flavio shouts, and Kim screams.

"Ouch! Hey!" Marple complains as Flavio lands on top of her.

"Ah, just where I'm supposed to be," Flavio grins, enjoying his overpowering position.

"Oh, shut up, you!" Marple nudges him. "Last in, first out is all I can say," she hisses back.

"Uh, I feel a little messed-up. Winston, can you see me?" Kim coughs. "Is my hair okay?" she asks, while trying to straighten herself.

"I wouldn't bother about it," Winston recommends. "The bag is nearly full. It can't be long before we'll be flying into the next container," he warns.

More peppers are dropped on top of them. Then nothing happens for a moment. The peppers can feel they are moving, but no new colleagues join them. Suddenly, everything happens quickly. Their bag is lifted upside down.

"Oi, I'm getting crushed!" Flavio complains, but nobody has time to answer. The bag is opened wide and they all go flying into a wooden crate. A lot of grumbling and cries of excitement follow each other.

"I think I have caught a splinter!" Kim screams over to Flavio.

"My dear, I'm lying at the bottom of a wooden crate, with hundreds of Pimientos de Padrón lying on top of me. I really have other problems," Flavio grunts back.

"Can you turn?" Winston asks her.

"I don't know, I feel a bit stuck," weeps Kim.

"Try to wriggle yourself a bit, maybe you'll turn," says Winston, trying to help.

"Uhhh," Kim moans.

"It's like belly dancing, it can't be that hard." Winston tries to motivate her. With watery eyes, Kim tries to do what she is told. She stretches her arms and slowly moves back and forth, turning a little every time she wriggles.

"Can you see anything?" she desperately asks.

"No, I can't, everything looks good from here. You probably just bumped yourself on the wood," Winston replies. "Ahhh, do you think I'll get a bruise? Nobody buys bruised vegetables!" she screeches, alarmed, making Winston role his eyes, but she cannot see it.

"No, no, you look fine. We won't be here for long. Surely we will be moving on soon," he says, calming her.

"Oh, that would be good, it's really hot here," Apollo whispers.

The hours creep on while the peppers lie in silence. Every now and then, a new wooden crate is balanced above the top one, and more and more peppers are poured inside. Dust crumbles through the cracks and covers their luscious coats. In the distance, they can hear the pickers happily singing and whistling while they make their way through the fields.

As Farmer Gonzales turns the key of his tractor, the trailer starts to vibrate to the rhythm of the engine. The moment has come - the Pimientos de Padrón are leaving their home fields. A wave of sadness shoots through them at the thought, but the thrill of anticipation wins the battle.

Their journey has begun!

Back in the fields, INNOCENCE, CLARITY and MARVELLOUS-ME don't let the trailer out of their sight. Parts of their souls have left. A world full of opportunities awaits them. It's an exciting and proud moment. They have produced the next generation, which will make the planet a better place.

And themselves? They will stay behind. Their reason for their being has been fulfilled. They will now age quickly and serve the next generation of homes of Pimientos de Padrón as soil fertilizer. But their existence will not have been in vain. They have produced wonderful peppers full of dreams, and their bodies will secure the generations to come. It has been a lot of hard work, but they wouldn't want to have missed a day of it. The three souls sincerely smile at each other, all knowing what's coming next.

One by one, they close their tired, but happy eyes and enjoy the last rays of sunlight in their short, but fulfilled lives.

*****

After a bumpy ride, the tractor and its trailer come to a sudden halt. The peppers can hear men speaking. The crates are quickly lifted from the trailer, carried into a shed and emptied into a metal container.

"Apollo, hold your breath!" Marple cries.

"Why? What's going on?" Apollo asks frantically.

"We're going to be washed. It's going to get wet for a short while. But we'll be okay. You hear!" Marple shouts.

The metal surface below them starts to move forward, and they gently vibrate to the sound of the machine's motor. Washing nozzles turn on in front of them. Cool water sprays down onto their bodies.

"This is fantastic!" Kim marvels, turning herself back and forth and rubbing her dusty body.

"Go for it, Apollo! Make the most out of it! Ensure you're really shiny and clean by the time we reach the end," she smiles with closed eyes. Apollo's first moment of shock declines, and he relaxes. This isn't that bad, he smiles to himself, and copies Kim's moves.

After three sets of washing nozzles, warm air is blown down from a large ventilator. The wet, shiny pearls are swept from their bodies. Apollo feels comfortably clean. He has actually never felt cleaner, and admiringly studies his body. His green coat shines wonderfully.

"Fantastic!" he shouts, quite to his own surprise, making Marple and Kim giggle.

"Looks like a pinch of MARVELLOUS-ME has rubbed off on you," Marple smiles.

"But look at us, we've never looked better," Apollo marvels, feeling proud of himself.

"Indeed, we all look marvellous," Kim gleams.

The moving surface below them comes to the end, and they are shoved onto a cool metal table.

"Ahhh!" Apollo gasps, seeing several pairs of dark brown eyes staring at them from above. A pair of hands comes down towards them, grabs a pile of peppers and gently places them into a crate with cardboard lining.

"Marple!" Apollo screams, desperately looking for his friends. "Don't worry, I'm here," Marple assures him.

"Ah, I am so happy, a soft lining. I couldn't take another bare, wooden crate," Kim sighs.

"They know where we belong," Flavio snorts. "This is only appropriate," he adds.

"Absolutely!" Kim agrees. "How else will I prepare for my life after this? I couldn't take another splinter or bump on my behind." She roles her eyes at the thought.

"Did anybody see the label on our box?" asks Winston, changing the subject to more important things. The peppers blink at each other, all desperate to hear whether anybody noticed.

"It was all a bit quick, I have to admit," Marple grumbles, realizing she'd missed the moment. "Oi, up there. Can you see the name of this box?" Marple shouts up to some peppers, lying above them. They all look at each other, waiting for a clever answer to pop-up. "Try and have a look through the gaps of the box, will you! Let me know if you can detect any letters," Marple carries on, commandingly. A pepper at the top of the box stretches himself to try and get a glimpse through the handle-holes of the box.

"The box next to us says something-something-something-DON. I can't see the first letters," the pepper shouts back.

"One of you, lift the poor fella, will you! We need to know the full name," Marple shouts back. Another pepper pushes himself beneath his colleague, to lift him higher up.

"Hold tight to my feet, I don't want to fall out," the daring pepper nervously requests. The pepper beneath him pushes and pushes until the pepper's head fully sticks through the boxes handle-hole.

"It says …ONDON. No, wait, there is something more. I need one more inch, guys," the pepper urges. The stretched pepper beneath him starts to jump to achieve the extra inch.

"ONDON …ONDON …ah, it says LONDON …" his voice echoes, followed by a screech as he loses balance. The jumping pepper below him stumbles and falls onto his back. The daring pepper vanishes through the box's handle-holes.

"Oh my God, he's fallen out of the box," Apollo gasps. "Hmm, well. Yes he has," Marple agrees, feeling unsure what to say.

"Woooohhh… Looondooon," the daring pepper screams, flying back into the box and landing on top of the pile. "My head! I've bumped my head," the pepper rubs himself. "Luckily one of the pickers saw me, and here I am, back in the box," he smiles.

"London! London!" Marple sings. "We are going to London, my friends," she smiles. "The first step of our destiny is already becoming reality," she gleams, hugging herself. Knowing their destination sparks excitement and dreams. London it will be!

Katherine Anne Lee

A long travel across the ocean awaits them. Tonight is their last night in the land of hopes and dreams of Pimientos de Padrón. They will breathe the fresh air of their fields and listen to the peacefulness of the valley just one more time.

The peppers lull themselves in the warm glow of their soul's land, the land of hopes and dreams of Pimientos de Padrón.

Vulnerable dreams 9

Things happen quickly the next day. The sun hasn't even risen when the lights go on in the shed. People are moving back and forth without much talk. A spirit of optimism lies in the air, and softly creeps into the crates.

"Oh, it's not even morning. What's going on?" Apollo moans.

"They're preparing for our departure," Marple gleams, fully awake.

"Shhh… I'm trying to sleep," Kim protests, turning to her side.

"Me too, but this noise," Apollo grumbles.

"Blend out the noise," Winston recommends.

"How can you blend out our departure? This is so exciting! Apollo, you've slept forever in the fields. Wake-up!" Marple beams. "London, here we come!" she shouts.

"Well done, now we're all awake," Flavio snorts, rubbing his eyes.

The crates around them are lifted and carried away one by one, allowing the shed's bright light to fill their temporary wooden home.

"We'll be next," Marple excitedly comments on the action.

"Some fresh air will be good! It's getting kind of warm in here," Flavio grunts.

"If you are truly planning on going to the south of Italy, you'd better get used to the heat," Marple recommends.

"I can bear the heat. What I meant was the stuffy air. The fields were hot, but the air was always fresh. It'll be similar down in the south of Italy. Hot, but always fresh ocean air," adds Flavio, explaining himself.

"Don't be too sure about that," Winston joins in. "My soul told me that the south of Italy has a waste disposal problem. Bags and bags of rubbish are lining the streets. Not the place for fresh air, my friend. And anyway, I'll be looking out for you. You'll be hiding in unpleasant places," Winston smiles, enjoying the thought of annoying Flavio.

"Well, I'll solve that problem. It'll be the first thing on my agenda. I'll have plenty of money, and it will be the least of my problems. And get off my back, don't you have better things to do than looking for me?" Flavio hisses.

"Okay, I'll let you solve some of the problems and then come after you," Winston laughs.

Their crate is lifted and carried outside. Fresh air wafts through the small openings of their wooden box. The early morning sun is just taking over the sky above the valley with the most beautiful red and yellow colours. A wonderful mix of brightness and warmth, wishing the peppers farewell.

The buzzing sound of a lorry's engine fills the air and causes the ground around them to tremble. Their transportation has arrived. The lorry's doors squeak, and hands are shaken, followed by some words of instruction. The crates are loaded and the lorry's heavy doors closed. In total darkness, the peppers tremble to the engine's rhythm, while they are driven away from the land of hopes and dreams of Pimientos de Padrón.

The peppers lie in silence while they travel. They have left their home, their place of origin. For the first time, they feel far away from their soul's home. New ways of connecting to their pod of knowledge need to be learned quickly. They have stored the essentials within them, but new situations will still require new knowledge. Concentration, feeling within themselves and deep belief in the sense of basic trust are required in order to grow further.

A tear of sadness runs down Apollo's cheek. It's not a conscious tear. It's the inner pain of detachment, squeezing his heart; releasing itself in a thick tear, running down the side of his face.

"Don't worry, Apollo," Marple whispers. "You're never detached. It's just different now. We have grown enough to be able to constantly be in touch with our soul, from wherever we are. Your soul of innocence will never leave you," she soothes.

"How do you know that I'm sad?", Apollo whispers back, feeling a little embarrassed that his emotional outbreak has been noticed in the pitch-black of the inside of the lorry.

"Because I feel it," Marple nudges him. "I used my capabilities to feel how the ones I care for are getting on. And okay, it is kind of obvious, isn't it!" she smiles genuinely.

"So how do I do this? How do I stay in contact with my soul?" Apollo asks.

"It's easy, you know what your soul feels like. Think of that feeling. Breathe deeply. Calm yourself, and then ask your question. Notice the feeling growing inside you, and identify its meaning. It takes a little practice, but believe me, everyone can do it!" Marple assures him. Apollo smiles and dries his tears. He loves Marple, she knows everything. What she says makes sense and is clear. She is a true soul of CLARITY. Her words are pure light, guiding him through the darkness.

After travelling for some time, the lorry stops and the engine is turned off. The peppers count the minutes of silence. In their perception of time, it could as well be hours of anticipation.

"Do you think we will be loaded into a flying machine?" Apollo asks excitedly.

"It's called an airplane," Winston corrects him.

"I know. But I like the name 'flying machine'. It's the first thing I learned about it, and it has stuck," says Apollo, defending his usage of words.

"As you wish," says Winston, raising his eyebrow. It's unusual for Apollo to defend himself.

"I don't think we will be flying, Apollo," Marple hesitantly answers him.

"So how are we getting to London?" Apollo asks in a disappointed tone.

"Next we will surely be loaded onto a boat," Winston informs him.

"A boat," Apollo repeats.

"Well, maybe it's a hovercraft. That would be very close to flying," he beams.

"I don't think so," Winston mutters. "Hovercrafts are not used that often, surely not to transport vegetables from A to B. But who knows, maybe I'm wrong," he says, rolling his eyes.

"If we don't travel on a hovercraft today, then I'll do it later on in my new life. Maybe I'll drive a hovercraft. I could become a hovercraft pilot," Apollo chats on, full of spirit.

"Now, that's an idea," adds Marple, cheering him up.

"In whatever way we travel, I just hope it's not too warm. I want to stay nice and firm. I mean, who's going to buy a shrivelled pepper?" Kim joins the discussion.

"I wouldn't worry about that. It's their priority to ensure we arrive looking well. They won't want to risk losing their pay. Wherever we are placed, it will surely be cooled down nicely," says Marple, explaining her thinking.

The doors of the lorry are flung open and the crates are quickly unloaded and piled into rows. The air is hot and the sun stands right above them, unmercifully demonstrating its strength. Marple, Apollo, Kim, Winston and Flavio's crate is on top of a pile, and they are ruthlessly exposed to the blazing rays of sunlight.

"Ah, this is deadly," Kim sighs. "I will dissolve any minute. Oi, somebody do something," she shouts to the busy workers. But her cry is unheard.

"Oh, look. Those crates over there are all labelled with London. They are being loaded onto that red boat. So it won't be long before we join them," Apollo observes happily.

One by one, the crates in front of them are lifted onto the boat and vanish into the darkness of the hold. After the last crate has been stored, the workers vanish, and the port goes quiet. Marple's group of peppers is left waiting in the blazing sun. Nobody seems to notice them.

"Something is wrong. We should have been loaded too," analyses Marple.

"Maybe we're going onto a different boat," Apollo comments naively.

"A different boat would mean a different location," Flavio cannot help a little sound of joy swinging in his words. "Maybe it's a direct ticket to Italy after all," he smirks.

"Don't be daft. I am sure the situation will become clear in a moment," says Marple, trying to sound convincing.

A new group of workers appear and examine the stacked crates. A man studies their label and shakes his head and shouts something to his colleague.

"Ha, see, he's noticed," Marple smiles. Their box is lifted and placed roughly on the ground with a bump. The workers quickly lift the other crates and carry them to a blue boat, which is anchored next to the red one. They are soon left all alone on the ground.

"Now what, clever clogs?" hisses Flavio. "We're all going to dry and shrivel away if we stay here any longer," he complains.

"Oh, this is not going according to plan. Am I already changing shape, Winston?" Kim wails, looking down at herself.

"Why are you always asking me? Ask your soul mate!" Winston answers, crossly. Their fear and the sun's heat is taking its toll, their mood is swinging.

Little, patting footsteps and heavy panting noises come close to their box. Suddenly, a wet, black nose appears above them. Dribble drops down onto the top peppers as the hairy creature sticks its nose into the pile of peppers. A foul smell of chewed leftovers and too little water is blown over their heads, followed by a spray of unwanted spit. The creature digs its nose even further into the peppers.

"Argh, it is coming closer," Kim gasps, trying to press herself over to Winston.

"Oh my God, what's this?" Apollo screams.

"It's a dog. Quite a dirty street dog. I don't think it will eat us peppers," Marple hopes.

"Ugh, if it doesn't eat us, surely its spit will make us go mouldy," Kim panics, protecting her head with her arms. "Keep your heads low! Luckily we're not on top of the pile," Marple commands.

The wet black nose goes on digging and comes dangerously close to Flavio.

"Ah, if it breaths at us again, I'm going to pass out," Flavio complains, turning his head away from the dog's mouth.

"Get used to the smell, my friend. Where you're going, it will be just like this until you get the rubbish problem under control," Winston grins, feeling out of danger.

The dog lifts its head for a moment, giving the peppers a second to breath. With its front paw, the dog digs around in the crate, pushing the peppers to one side. Its brown claws dangerously stab past the peppers. Any moment one of them could be speared, meaning a sure and dreadful death.

"Get away, you beast!" Flavio swears at the dog's paw. "I'll be back to finish with you. You just wait!" he carries on, shouting at the dog's dirty feet. Disappointed, the dog pulls its paw back and studies the area.

"Ha, that's what I mean. Don't mess with me!" Flavio proudly cheers, lifting his fist in victory. "As long as you're with me, the Padre, you're safe!" he proudly explains, opening his arms as if to cuddle the peppers. Before he can return his hands back to the side of his body, the dog digs its nose into the pile of peppers again. It opens its mouth, exhaling a deadly smell, and snaps one of the peppers with its dirty teeth. All gasp in shock.

Outside the crate, the dog drops the poor pepper onto the hot tarmac. The unlucky pepper squeals in horror to his colleagues, but there's nothing they can do.

Without hesitating, the dog's head dives down after the pepper. The despairing cries of the pepper echo through the air as the dog lifts its head. Watery spit runs down the dog's jaw as it bites and chews the pepper's body. Frozen to the spot, the peppers in the crate watch their colleague close his eyes while losing his life to this ugly creature.

But the dog isn't pleased with its catch and, irritated, it shakes its head, spitting the remains of the pepper to the ground. The action is followed by a sore cough and choking sound, as the dog splutters its insides out.

"That will teach you!" Flavio shouts. "A hot one! You got a hot one, didn't you?" Flavio loudly laughs. The other peppers look at him in shock. "What? What's now? We survived, didn't we? The hot pepper sacrificed himself for us to live on. Life isn't always fair. Life's not always a merry playground. Get used to it!" Flavio snorts at the crowd of widened eyes.

"You could be a bit more politically correct," Kim whispers to her soul mate, Flavio. "That was kind of ruthless. You could have given us a minute," she purrs.

"I don't think we should be cheering too much. We're still lying here in the hot sun. It's not as though we're already loaded onto our boat. Our dreams are still in danger," Marple calmly reminds them.

"What if the dog comes back? Maybe it wants a second try," says Apollo, expressing his fear. The peppers look at the dog, which is still shaking his head and spitting on the ground.

"You're right. I'm sure it doesn't have an elephant's brain. It will most probably be back as soon as the shock has faded," Marple realises, a little worried by her own words.

Their worries are scattered by a sharp whistle. A man with heavy boots runs towards the dog, shouting and wildly waving his arms. The dog quickly lifts its head and starts to run. With his hands on his hips, the man studies the abandoned box of Piementos de Padrón. He finally picks it up and checks the label.

"Please, please, let him notice where we belong," Marple prays aloud. All the peppers join in, and squeeze their eyes closed in anticipation.

The man looks left and right, and finally whistles over to the red boat. A short man with a woolly hat appears at the boat's railing. In loud voices, they exchange some words and the man, holding the crate of peppers, shows him the box.

"Come on, come on. Pass us over. We need to be on board," Marple pleads. The man at the railing scratches his head and then kneels down with stretched arms. The crate of peppers is passed over and within minutes, they are stored below deck.

"Oh, we've made it. We've made it!" Marple cries out loud and the other peppers join in.

"We're safe," Kim sobs, combing her hair and resting her back against Winston.

After they have all have calmed down, Apollo can't hold back his thoughts anymore.

"Marple, what do you think has happened to that poor pepper?" he asks in a quiet voice. Marple rubs her face. "Hmm, well, I think he was just not meant to be eaten. He can be glad that this dirty creature didn't swallow him. Imagine waking up as that dog!" she scowls. "I think his meaning in life was to save us," she thoughtfully adds after a minute's pause. "If that pepper hadn't have been here, we all would have been lost. Imagine all the destroyed and wasted dreams," Marple carries on.

"But what about his dreams?" Apollo persists.

"He was a soul of shelter. He dreamt of protecting the less fortunate," a pepper above them sobs. Apollo's jaw drops at his words. "His faith has been fulfilled, I guess," the pepper rubs his eyes.

"I would say it has," Winston agrees.

"I don't like being regarded as the less fortunate," Flavio pouts.

"Oh, shut-up! You should be thankful. Thankful to the pepper and faith, who made sure we had a protecting hand over us," Marple tells him off. The peppers go quiet and give their minds a moment to work out the recent event.

Away from the land of hopes and dream of Pimientos de Padrón, the peppers are faced with their first life-threatening event. Without Farmer Gonzales protecting them, they are vulnerable. Their belief in faith and the world's good will is their essential asset.

Hopes and dreams suddenly take unexpected turns. Turns they had not thought about, but that now seem very explainable. A dream is a dream. But is every dream laid out and considered in every form that it could take?

While the peppers rest in the dim light of the boat's hold, the sun creeps along the sky and dries the remains of the ones who have sacrificed themselves so that others can survive. The soul's meaning is individual. While some share a common purpose, it can come to pass in unexpected ways. Of one thing we can be sure, however: the soul will always fulfil its very own, engraved destiny.

Back in the land of hopes and dreams of Pimientos de Padrón, the pepper's souls wish them well, whatever path their destiny chooses to take.

Butterflies of our life 10

After some cooling-down in the boat's air-conditioned hold, the peppers fall into a restless sleep. The smell of the stray dog's breath and its dirty nose burying into their crate has burned itself into their minds. Seeing their co-pepper being splattered over the hot tarmac cannot be let go so easily, even though they know the techniques for releasing unwanted experiences. They are masters at cutting off bad balloons that they have unintentionally picked-up, and finding their way back to their purest soul. Coming to terms with the gruesome pictures will take some healing.

The cool air of the boat's hold smells of old wood mixed with a metallic scent of the busily running engines. A well-trained nose could possibly even detect a fine trace of motor oil. But it could just as well be the brain interfering, with knowledge and expectations of finding such a scent.

The engines hum as the boat puts out to sea, and the peppers sway to the ocean's waves. Their shiny coats gently rub against each other, quite to the liking of Kim. She likes to be back-to-back with Winston and he secretly enjoys her closeness. Two very different souls, that wonderfully harmonize if they want to. By pretending to sleep, Winston can lie back and enjoy her company, without having to complain about something. Kim softly purrs in her sleep.

"Look at those two lovebirds," Marple whispers to Apollo. "Who would have thought," she muses with a smile.

"They look very comfortable," Apollo whispers back, enjoying the sight of unity. "They do, as long as they're asleep," Marple pouts. "Awake, they will probably never make it," she adds.

"Why not? Wouldn't it be nice to have two of our row find each other?" Apollo gleams.

"Ha! We are on our way to our destiny. We'll then be eaten and become human. There is not much time to bill and coo. They can do that to their full extent once they're human," Marple grumbles, feeling a little left out.

"Oh, do you think they will find each other again when they are humans," Apollo excitedly asks. His spirit lifts at the thought.

"Find each other? I don't know. I haven't thought of it. I guess it's possible. Yes, why not. But I don't think they would be the most harmonious match. They do have quite different destinies," Marple works on the thought.

"You two, hold it there. My soul mate, Kim, will not join up with your Winston. I mean, think of it! That would mean I'd have to put up with him, and we two are definitely not on the same path of destiny," says Flavio, interrupting their ideas.

"Actually, I thought that you two are. You will be down south living the life of a Godfather, and he will be after you. You two have been on about it the whole summer." Marple rolls her eyes.

"Well, maybe we will. But Kim will surely not be accompanying him in doing that. So that's it!" Flavio sharply returns. "But wait a minute, maybe she should. She could make sure he never really makes it. Lead him onto the wrong path, if you know what I mean. Hmm, I'm quite liking the thought," Flavio smiles evilly.

"You're disgusting, really. I don't understand where you get it all from. It can't possibly all be in that little body of yours," Marple hisses.

"Now then, we all know better than that. I don't like that tone of yours," says Flavio, enjoying himself, while Apollo can hardly hold himself back.

"I believe in love. You can be marvellous and lovely. That's what Kim will be. Maybe their paths will turn out to be totally different. Maybe they will have wonderful children and Winston will be a lawyer or something, and not want to be actively chasing the bad side. They will have a marvellous home, in a grand city. Everyone will be happy." Apollo smiles a dreamy smile.

Flavio lifts an eyebrow and snorts. "You're getting a bit carried away, my little friend," he replies dryly, but Apollo doesn't mind. He is already picturing the innocent life they could be living, with a speck of glamour.

Flavio starts to push himself forward, causing other peppers to complain.

"Arrg, your sweet thoughts are bothering me, Apollo. Stop that, will you! I can feel them all over. It's annoying! It's making me twitch," Flavio complains.

"Feeling uncomfortable, are you?" laughs Marple, enjoying herself. "Keep on going, Apollo! This pepper needs a bit of pink potion to lighten him up," she grins.

"Cool it down, both of you! I'm feeling sick," Flavio shouts.

"What's going on?" Winston grumbles, opening his eyes.

"Nothing," Apollo spits out in surprise.

Winston stretches himself and tries to casually move away from Kim. "Well, it doesn't sound like nothing. What are you three on about? We should be resting." Winston tries again.

"Some of us are resting wonderfully," Marple smirks.

"Oh we are," Kim smiles with closed eyes. I was feeling really comfortable. Why have you moved away, Winston?" she asks, patting her back, as if to say "please move back". Marple and Apollo can't help but giggle.

"I think you're all getting carried away." Winston analyses their behaviour with an inspecting look.

"Whatever. Apollo, stop thinking what you're thinking. It's making me feel sick!" Flavio grumbles, holding his tummy.

"I'm not feeling that well either," a pepper next to Flavio admits.

"Ah, see! Do you see what you're doing to us all, Apollo?", Flavio complains sharply, feeling a little lifted, not being the only one touched by so much love.

"How do you know what I'm thinking about?" asks Apollo, feeling perplexed about causing sick tummies.

"Because I can feel it. I'm very skilled, that's why it hit me first. Look how I'm twitching. If you carry on, we'll all soon be feeling bad. With some it just takes a bit longer," Flavio hisses.

"So, what am I thinking about?" Apollo wants to know, still not understanding what apparently terrible thing he is doing.

"Arrgh, butterfly things. I really don't want to go into details. I'm feeling sick enough without speaking out the words." Flavio moans in agony.

"Butterfly stuff? I was thinking of a life in love. Finding your missing piece and then meeting again after you've reached your higher meaning. How powerful would that be? How high could you fly? No air machine would be needed. Their own wings will take them. Two souls of the future generation, meeting after their transformation and continuing their love story. The world would lie at their feet and the clouds would carry them. Every step a gentle jump and a soft landing. Always together. In the past. In the present. And in the future," says Apollo, proudly expressing his thoughts.

"That's wonderful. Maybe you should become a writer instead of a flying machine or hovercraft pilot," nods Kim, admiringly congratulating him on his words.

"Whoa, that's it. Everything has gone sour in my mouth," Flavio blurts out, feeling his stomach churning as the boat gently sways to one side.

"I only wanted to express that I'm not thinking of butter-flies, but of an extraordinary life in love," explains Apollo.

"Apollo, if you feel overwhelming love, how would you describe it?" Marple asks him.

"It's a tingling in my tummy. As if I had swallowed a fizzy tablet," he smiles, enjoying the thought.

"Some people describe that feeling as butterflies flapping their wings in their stomach," Marple smiles.

"Oh, so the butterflies stand for feeling love. I like that!" Apollo shyly giggles.

"Yeah, but some of us don't," Flavio tells him in a sharp tone.

"Guys, really! Calm down! We're on a boat that has set sail. We're somewhere on the ocean. There are waves that are making our boat sway. Think about it! It's not Apollo's pink thinking that is making you feel bad. You're seasick!" Marple winks, getting fed-up of the never-ending discussion.

"Who knows? I'm a private-jet kind of guy. I'm not built to be on a boat. Okay, maybe a luxury yacht in the Bay of Costa Smeralda, but that's another story," Flavio defends himself.

"Oh, Costa Smeralda. I'll be there," Kim excitedly squeals.

"No you won't, not with him," Flavio pouts.

"Not with whom?" Kim asks, feeling surprised.

"Him of course. Your Mr Butterfly," Flavio gestures in an Italian manner, all over the place.

"Your boat butterflies are making you weird," Kim roles her eyes at him, and looks for Winston's back to lean on.

"Anyway, you and all others that are feeling sick should get to the side of the crate before your boat butterflies decide to escape all over us," Marple points with her index finger. "I'm not having any of you being sick all over me," she sharply explains her thinking. The pepper next to Flavio quickly moves to the side. He is too afraid of Marple's sharp tongue. But Flavio wouldn't have been himself if he had moved. He only turns to his side and cradles his tummy, ignoring her words.

"How long will we be on here, anyway," he mumbles. "A couple of days I'd guess," Winston reckons, leaning back on Kim.

Butterflies of all kinds have sneaked on board the boat's hold. Some peppers feel sick, others confused. Two haven't placed them yet, and one has already guided them all the way down the altar.

Tingling sensations can be hard to place, and are not always welcomed by the world they invade. Deep within, the soul is keeping its promise and sending its most delicate and beautiful creature to torment the feelings. As the butterflies flap their fine, powdery wings, destiny unfolds itself. New paths open and other souls join the journey. Some only for a short time, while others join forever and never truly leave the heart they have entered. Their delicate being and their honest love is comparable with a butterfly's wing. Overflowing with beauty, nature's prodigy and highly vulnerable.

As the butterflies flap their powdery wings, hopes and dreams of Pimientos de Padrón shower down and softly coat the future generation, like icing on a cake.

Our karma in a rainbow of light

11

The night sky peers through the dull glass of the hold's portholes. The first stars are out, but it's impossible to gaze at them. It looks as though the stars are shooting back and forth across the sky, but it's actually the porthole that is moving up and down. It's the peppers' first night on board, and the ocean is not showing itself from its best side. The boat has sailed into some bad weather.

"Uhhh, this is not getting any better. I feel awful," Flavio complains, cuddling himself.

"Get over to the side of the crate. I've already told you," Marple commands, but Flavio is much too concerned with his own being, and just ignores her. The other sick pepper is clutching to the wooden handle holes of the box, not looking very good.

"If I wasn't naturally green, I definitely would be now," grumbles Flavio.

"Flavio, I'm really sorry I can't help you. I would feel more comfortable though, if you could move away from me. Just a little. Only for the night, you know," Kim pleads.

"You're all monsters. You only think of your own good. And what about me? Your Godfather. How would you have liked it if I had moved away from you when we were out there in the burning sun with this smelly dog, digging his nose into our crate? I protected all of you. I did. I truly did, and this is your way of thanking me? Nothing but constant nagging. Why isn't anyone rubbing my back?" Flavio sulks. Outside, a vicious wind picks up and whips water against the ship's bow. Their crate moves dangerously to one side and some loose pieces roll across the boats hold floor and slam against the wooden walls.

"Ahhh, I can't hold myself," some peppers squeal and tumble over to the momentarily lower side of the crate, squashing other peppers.

"Hold on to each other! Build a chain!" Marple shouts, stretching out to Apollo and another pepper. Some do as they are told, but the majority are too afraid to move.

"Kim, hold my hand," Flavio angrily shouts at his soul mate.

"I don't know, maybe it's better if you roll over a little. You'll be closer to the edge. You know, in case you get sick," she fidgets, not feeling sure about what she should do.

"This isn't an option I'm offering you. Take my hand!" Flavio screams at her, going red.

"Okay, okay, calm down. You don't need to get so upset." Kim obeys, offering him her hand and clutching Winston with the other. More water is whipped against the other side of the boat and their crate sways to the other side.

Upstairs, they can hear heavy boots running across the floor. The crew is in action, something is going on.

"It's probably only a bad patch of weather. All will be over soon," says Marple, trying to calm everyone. More peppers are hurled to the other side of the crate this time, bumping the sick pepper. The swaying game carries on and picks up speed. They are swayed rhythmically from one side to the other. Through the portholes, the stars in the sky shoot up and down, drawing illuminated tails behind them. Now and then, the water's cold fingers hit loudly against the glass, leaving aggressive-looking splashes of water, which break up into little water pools in the next minute, and roll to the other side of the window. It feels as if two sea monsters are playing with the boat. A game of water tennis, and the boat is their vibrant, felt ball.

Water leaks from somewhere into the hold, and gurgles along the side of the boat. The next time they are thrown to the other side, the gurgling salty water splashes through the air and wets their little bodies.

"Oh, this is getting too much. I feel so bad," the sick pepper cries, pushing himself up and sticking his head out of the crate's handle hole. From deep down, a burp escapes his lips. He just manages to gasp some air before his stomach empties itself. The pepper desperately grabs the sides of the handle hole as the next wave of sickness overcomes him, and it all happens again.

Salt water splashes his face and washes away his stomach's remains. Like a drowned rat, he hangs his head over the side of the crate and desperately gasps for air. His throat is burning and a foul smell creeps up his nose.

The boat starts to sway to the other side again. The sick pepper can see the ground coming closer and closer. Trying to avoid further dizziness, he closes his eyes and swallows heavily. Unsecured peppers start to slide towards the lower side of the crate, screaming as they bump into each other.

A chain reaction cannot be stopped. All the peppers move in synchronisation with the boat. One loose pepper bumps another, eventually sending the last one in the chain flying towards the backside of the sick pepper, who is hanging his head out of the crate.

With a scream of surprise, the sick pepper is shot out of the crate, like a bullet out of a gun.

"Oh my God! Oh my God!" the accidental perpetrator squeals, covering his eyes with his hands.

"I told you! I told you! Now see what's happened," Marple angrily scolds. "You should be hanging on to each other," she glares at them.

"Oops, another one bites the dust," Flavio dryly comments.

"You watch it. You should be over there too," Winston glares.

"Ha, that is exactly why I'm not there. You guys would have probably gave me an extra push," Flavio proudly exclaims.

"I probably would have. It would save me some work in my future life," Winston hits back.

"Calm down! There's nothing we can do. He's gone. Hold on to each other. We will be swaying back to the other side any minute," Kim pleas.

Far below the stacked crates, the sick pepper lands in a pool of salty water, which breaks his fall. As soon as his little body touches the wooden ground, the boat moves to the other side, and he is swirled across the floor. Other unrecognizable, loose objects follow him. Together, they are slammed against the boat's wall.

Due to his light weight, he manages to stay just above the surface, gasping for air. Again and again he is washed from one corner to the other.

This must be it, he thinks, feeling pity and uselessness of his pure being building up inside.

He lands in the next corner, the water curdling and bubbling around him. Something is sucking and pulling him in one direction. The sound of screaming water deafens his ears. It's as if the water is fighting against whatever is sucking it up. The sickness and the fall has robbed all his energy, he just lets himself go, accepting all that is coming to him. It can't get any worse, he reckons.

Like a leaf in the water, he sails towards the loud churning sound. Within split seconds he is sucked into a tube. He is bumped against a plastic pipe several times, and then ungracefully spat out of the other side.

The pepper is hurdled out of the boat, right into the arms of the wave. White foam builds around him, laying him in a soft cushion of bubbles that climb up the side of the boat. A second later the wave pulls back and its greedy fingers dig down into the ocean to build more power.

The pepper is swirled around in the ocean's washing machine.

Once again he is spat to the surface and slammed against the boat, foam cradling his body. The water's power robs the pepper's last breath. His body sags and he lets his head go, as he sways into unconsciousness. Like a child that has lost interest in a toy, the waves drop the pepper and lets him sink below their rumbling surface.

Lifeless, the pepper sinks through the water. His eyes are closed and little bubbles of air escape his mouth. All his thoughts are gone. All is calm and quiet. No fear chokes his mind.

A sudden bump in his stomach wakes him up and slams him ruthlessly back into reality. Coughing heavily, he turns to each side and squeals into the darkness of the water.

Salty fluid fills his mouth and lungs. The echo of his scream bounces off the walls of his mind, but doesn't travel outside his body. The compact water suppresses all sound. A camouflage-coloured creature swims away from him into the deep blue. The fish's calm movements make its travel seem so effortless. Every time it moves its tail to one side, a gentle push of water flows towards the pepper, making him spin around his own axis.

The dark blue swirls around him and little bubbles cloud his view. The invading, salty water and his mortal agony send him back into unconsciousness. His body flakes back and his little arms dangle into the unknown, while he slowly sways deeper and deeper into the ocean. With every inch he travels, the water thickens and the colours darken.

The seemingly lifeless pepper attracts the attention of a school of fish. Carefully they swim around the peculiar vegetable, occasionally bumping him with their tails. One of the fish takes a chance, and nibbles the pepper's finger. The others join in quickly, not wanting to miss out on a bite. The tickling sensation awakens the pepper back to life.

Flat, round eyes stare at him in shock. A pair of soft, thick lips are sucking the back of his hand. He can feel little sharp teeth scratching the surface of his shiny coat. It's a tickle that is starting to go a little too far. Annoyed, the pepper shakes his hand, knocking off the too-daring fish. The school simultaneously bounces back in surprise. They were not expecting the vegetable to come alive. But their curiosity overcomes them and they sneakily close their lines again.

"Oi, get a life. I'm not your dinner," the pepper shouts at them, holding his index finger up. His voice is deep and the flow of his words is delayed in time. But they don't miss their meaning. The school backs off again. Unsure if they should leave or stay, they scatter some distance around the pepper.

"I mean it! Hit the road!" the pepper warns, placing his hands on his hips, trying to look angry and overpowering. Amused by his own deep voice, he shouts a few more warning words and giggles to himself.

The school of fish chooses not to take any risk, turns and quickly vanishes into the dark.

Left alone, the pepper leans back into a see-through water cushion and gazes at the dark-blue water. He is not sure if he is still sinking. But he must be, the dark-blue is turning into a pitch-black. In slow motion, he waves his hand through the water above him. Glittery pearls follow his arm. The rainbow of light awakens amazement and feelings of thankfulness for the miracle of life within him.

Deep-sea drunk, the pepper falls through layers of water into the unknown. Fascinated by the sensation, he waves his arms back and forth and gazes at the self-made meteor shower following his arms with widened eyes and open mouth.

Drugged by the beauty and the growing water pressure, he throws his head back and laughs hysterically. In the timelessness of being, he travels through peaceful space. Only his own laughter echoes in his mind.

After what could have been hours of lost time in delirium, his back touches soft sand. Smoothly, his body bounces onto the bottom of the ocean. The surroundings are pitch-black.

"Ah, I've arrived at my destination," the pepper giggles, and strokes the cushion beneath him. Fine, powdery sand rises around him and tickles his nose. Otherwise nothing changes, nothing else happens.

The pepper rests on his back in silence. Is this it? He wonders and tries to turn to his side. The thickness of the water makes it difficult to move. He presses his little feet into the sand and struggles himself onto his stomach. The powdery ground rises and goes right up his nose, leaving him coughing and sneezing. Suddenly, the ground beneath him starts to move.

"Wow, I am on a flying carpet," the pepper squeals with joy.

With one hit he is flipped into the air. Ruggedly, he lands back on the ground.

"Uff!" he moans. "What was that?" he shouts into the dark. There is no reply, only his own voice echoing in his mind.

But he's not alone. From behind, a pair of dark eyes focus on him. His karma is sealed with one sharp and precise movement.

The sunken pepper is gone.

A few self-made shooting stars whiz through the water, sink and fade on touching the sand. Nothing is left that could prove the pepper had ever been here. No evidence of a Pimientos de Padrón ever touching such a depth.

At a first glance, one Pimientos de Padrón has been caught by less fortunate karma. Were his hopes and dreams not fulfilled?

Will his journey carry on at the bottom of the ocean, to a place never seen before by a Pimientos de Padrón?

New angles and options open. A soul in the valley of hopes and dreams of Pimientos de Padrón is fed with new impressions and knowledge, which will be shared for generations to come.

*****

The morning sun shines into the hold through the murky portholes. The boat has sailed into calmer waters. All is quiet. The boat's crew snore peacefully upstairs. It was a long night fighting against the storm. Downstairs, in the hold, the pumps gurgle, sucking up the last remains of salty water and transporting it back into the ocean.

Jumbled up, the peppers rest in their wooden crate. Heads and feet randomly lean against each other. Faint breathing witnesses their survival, while they calmly travel towards their destination.

"Hmm, Apollo, is that your toe sticking up my nose?" Marple complains, grasping for breath. Nobody moves.

"Uff, whoever this belongs to, move!" Marple sharply commands, getting annoyed. Still nobody moves. Marple swipes out with her arm and slaps the foot in her face, making Apollo scream.

"Ouch, Marple! Why are you doing that?" Apollo cries.

"Do you think it's fun having your smelly toe up my nose? I did tell you to move," Marple sharply explains her doing.

"I'm a sleeper. It's been a long night, and if that's not enough, you also make it a short morning. You could have gently moved aside," Apollo grumbles, turning to his side, and pulling his knees up to his tummy.

"You're such a baby. You should be up and excited. We'll be landing soon," Marple sparkles.

"I don't know. I don't think we can be sure of ourselves yet. Look what happened to that poor sick pepper. The same could happen to us today," Apollo shivers, not feeling excited at all.

"You don't know what happened to him. He's probably totally fine," says Marple, trying to lighten the discussion.

"Do you think so?" Apollo quietly asks, rubbing his shins. "I wish it wasn't so cold," he complains.

"Yes, I think he is," Marple smiles.

"So what do you think happened to him after he fell out of the crate?" Apollo asks.

"Hmm, listening to the sound of the water pumps, I think he isn't on the boat anymore," Marple lifts an eyebrow knowingly.

"Really!" Apollo gasps. He had heard the engine noises, but hadn't been able to place them. He was too caught up with the happenings to think about them any further.

"So where is he now?" he asks.

"Well somewhere in the ocean, obviously," Marple answers, a little irritated by the question. "Oh, yes. The ocean, of course," Apollo repeats, pretending to rub something off his legs. "So what is he doing in the ocean?" Apollo nonchalantly asks.

"Swimming with the dolphins," Kim proposes.

"Swimming with dolphins! I like that." Apollo's eyes go all dreamy and glazed.

"Pfft, swimming with the dolphins. Come on! He's sunk like a stone," Flavio laughs nastily. "He's building sandcastles at the bottom of the ocean. Get real," he adds, with another deep chuckle.

"I wouldn't be too sure about that! My soul tells me something else. He's taken another path, that's all," Marple tells Flavio.

"Apollo, you and I can go with the dolphin version. I like that. It's so romantic," Kim smiles, peering up at Winston through her thick eyelashes. Winston proudly grins down at her.

"What I believe has happened is quite similar. You're not far off," Marple carries on, rolling her eyes at the sight of the two lovebirds.

"So, what do you think has happened, Marple?" Apollo asks.

"Well, it was a vicious storm. He has had to go through some levels of water to reach calmer shores. And now, now I believe he has become an ocean's living being. Imagine the space and depth he now has around him. He can travel the world by water. The detour he has chosen isn't that bad, I think," she smiles.

"The detour," Apollo repeats. "Do you think many more of us need to take it?" he asks.

"Who knows? The protecting hand of our home lies far behind us. So many unexpected things can still happen. But we are close. I can feel it in my bones," Marple assures.

"Our home's protecting hand was not a sure value, my dear. Remember the fire," Winston reminds her.

"Yes, you're right. The fire. The poor, old oak tree. But still, Farmer Gonzales was there and protected us from worse," Marple reminds.

"I know what you want to say, Marple. We don't need to be afraid. There is always the unexpected positive in everything," Apollo sincerely smiles at her. All the peppers nod and admiringly smile back at Apollo.

The day after the storm remains calm. On board, a thankful and forgivable spirit spreads. Hopes and dreams are not buried out of fear.

Katherine Anne Lee

Change happens, and paths take new turns. Nothing is embedded in concrete. Some dreams are let go to open doors to new ones.

While the peppers rest, the protecting hand of the land of the hopes and dreams of Pimientos de Padrón guides their voyage.

Arriving and remembering 12

The day of their arrival begins really, really early. Their boat anchors before the sun rises. A light layer of mist calmly floats above the water's surface and enchantingly dances around the bow of the boat. The land is officially still in the middle of its summer time, but the half-way point has already been reached, and the days are consequently slowly shortening their allowance of sunlight. It's a mystical moment of silence, peacefully waiting for the day to awaken.

Marple is up first. Her strong link to her inner soul of CLARITY enables her to know what's happened. Even though locked in a dark hold, she knows with certainty that they have arrived. Their journey is approaching its last lap.

"Apollo!" she nudges. "Wake up! The boat has anchored. We've arrived," she whispers excitedly, with large, dazzling eyes.

"Oh Marple, it was so peaceful. Why are you waking me? It's still dark," Apollo grumbles, and turns onto his other side.

"Come on. Rub your eyes. Get ready! They will unload us soon. This is so exciting!" she squeals with happiness.

"What's all this noise, Marple?" Winston asks, stretching his body.

"We've arrived in good old England. Our home to be. I can feel it. Haven't you noticed that the ship isn't sailing anymore? We're standing still," Marple smartly explains.

"We've arrived! Oh my God! Oh my God, I must tidy myself up," Kim screeches, suddenly totally awake and fidgety.

"You look fine, don't worry about it," replies Winston smoothly.

"You must be kidding! After all these days of being in this fridge, rocked all over the place with all sorts of body pieces punching me. There's no way that I look fine! And anyway, fine is not good enough. I need to shine. This is it; our final destination," Kim protests, while nervously combing her hair with her fingers.

"I am just so glad I have my colour back in time. Imagine if the sea would have stayed so stormy. Who would have bought a pale pepper? Imagine arriving at your destiny and then nobody eats you," Flavio grunts.

"Who would have thought that Pimientos de Padrón could be seasick," Winston chuckles, remembering Flavio's colourless face, wrinkled with worry.

"Do you think we'll remember all of this after we've been eaten? I would love to pull your leg about it once I catch you," Winston teases.

"Do you think we won't remember each other after our dream has fulfilled? asks Apollo.

"Hmm, that's a good question," Marple wrinkles her brows.

"So what do you think?" insists Apollo.

"Well, thinking of the process, we're entering a new life. A new body with so many more options. I think we will just be overwhelmed by it all. But we will have the needed preconditions to remember and to reach deep into our soul. I think we'll feel a connection, but it will be difficult to place it, as we will be so occupied with new things and impressions."

"I don't need to remember. I'll be fine without all of you. Really sorry, but my life will be filled to the fullest. Neither time nor need to reach within me and remember this. Why would I?" Flavio bluntly gestures around him.

"Come on! Don't be so superficial. Of course you will remember me, my dearest," Kim purrs.

"Normally, yes. I would always spot a soul of MARVELLOUS-ME from miles away. But you've been heading in a strange direction lately. I'm not sure it's a good idea to stay in contact. You're surrounded by too much CLARITY for my taste," Flavio bluntly replies.

"Why would you say that? You are so cruel! We're from the same soul, the same seed's dream. We, Flavio, will never be far apart, whether you like it or not. No is an answer I will not accept," Kim pouts. "Anyway, I don't have time to debate with you," she adds, and turns away, busily smoothing her skin and hair.

Flavio just roles his eyes. "Women!" he mumbles between his teeth.

"Marple, I'll always stay in contact with you," Apollo whispers, looking up at her. "What do you think all these new things are that will occupy us so much?" he adds, feeling excitement building up inside of him.

"You know, humans are very distracted with all that's going on around them. Tons of things block their vision of true life," Marple explains with a creased forehead.

"Oh yes, electronic gadgets. I have learned all about them," Winston butts in. "I want one of these flat-screen phones that you can operate with only the tip of your finger. Very neat and smart! Imagine, Apollo, you can track down whatever you want with an electronic map on your hand-held," Winston smiles with a wink.

"Oh yes, I will need one of those to guide me through the air in my flying machine or across the water in my hovercraft. Can you get bigger ones? I think I need a bigger one because my rides could be quite bumpy. The ocean is not a thing to play with, as we've learned," comments Apollo, thinking of the stormy night they experienced.

"They're called pads. You just get yourself a pad and you'll be fine. If you decide to be my private jet pilot, I will make sure you have one on board," Flavio generously gestures.

"So you will remember me!" Apollo gasps in excitement.

Flavio wasn't expecting such a comment. "No, obviously not. It will be standard equipment on board my jet. The newest of the new. The MARVELLOUS-ME jet will not lack any gadgets," Flavio bluntly replies after a few seconds. Flavio wouldn't be Flavio if he didn't have an impersonal answer ready.

"I don't know, I think you'll remember me," Apollo smiles sincerely, not letting Flavio take away the happiness he feels.

"I will have a flat-screen phone too. I've heard that you can press a button and the gadget's screen turns into a mirror. Just what a girl of the world needs. God, I wish I had one here," Kim sighs.

"Anyway, Apollo, as you see, these things and many others cloud the human's vision. That's why you have to be careful with such things. There's too much connection to everything. Most of it is not needed. Just remember that," Marple tells them with a serious look. "We're all already connected to the earth without all that stuff, and it works fine," she adds.

"Some more, some less. You're Apollo's flat-screen phone, let's face it. He'll need one of those things once he's back on earth as a human without you," Flavio laughs.

"No he won't! He can have one, but he doesn't have to. I've taught him on our travels. Apollo will be fine, standing on his own two feet. He just has to be careful about listening to people like you," Marple sharply answers, turning to Apollo with a "do you hear me" look.

"Don't worry Marple, I'm a soul of INNOCENCE. I listen to everything, take in many impressions and am open to learn and experience. That's why I sometimes take an extra turn. But my basic trust will always lead me the right way. I know I'll remember you all. I look forward to that moment of memory," Apollo smiles happily. None of the peppers can deny an inner feeling of joy listening to Apollo's words.

Their moment of silence is broken as the doors to the hold fly open. Lights go on, heavy boots march in and a deep voice sharply gives commands to the workers, while pointing around the room. Stacks of crates are lifted, one at a time, and carried out of the hold by strong men.

Waiting their turn, the Pimientos de Padrón hold on to each other and watch the other vegetables leave. Baby lettuces and carrots are carried out into the fresh air. Their stack will be next.

A worker wearing a smudged white t-shirt walks up to the Pimientos de Padrón crates and lifts the top five. He breathes heavily, exhaling a smell of coffee and tobacco, while carrying them up the stairs. His skin is greasy and smells of motor oil and sweat.

Kim squints her eyes and claps her hands over her little nose. "Air! Air! I need air," she screeches, while Marple quietly counts the steps the worker is climbing up.

After reaching the entrance to the hold, they're swiftly carried through a narrow passageway, up some more steps and then out into the fresh, salty air. The sun is just tickling the horizon and illuminating the harbour with its first welcoming, bright yellow rays of light. A light breeze sways through the anchoring boats, bringing the untouched air from the ocean. It's a welcoming treat for the Pimientos de Padrón. A gush of childhood memories of hanging in the lanes of hopes and dreams, feeling the fresh air tickle their little bodies. And now so much has happened, they've come so far, experienced so much, lost friends and companions. Their hopes and dreams seem only a small step away, nearly touchable, an invading scent that cannot quite be reached just yet.

Their stack of crates are dropped onto a wooden pallet with a bump. The smudgy white T-shirt worker quickly heads off back to the boat. Other crates are stacked high to the left and right of them.

"Oyeh, now in the morning light I can at last see you guys," shouts a green baby lettuce over to their box. The Pimientos de Padrón look at each other in surprise.

"What was that? Did somebody say something?" Marple finally asks the peppers, a little puzzled.

"I said something. I said I can finally see you, my neighbour," the lettuce chuckles. "I was wondering who's next to us," the lettuce carries on.

"Is that green elephant ear talking to us?" asks Flavio, scrunching his nose.

"Oh that's a good one. You know elephants, do you?" the lettuce replies in a voice that doesn't seem very bothered.

"I know they exist in some countries. Around here they live in zoos, and like eating lettuce. Maybe you'll get to know them a little closer soon," Flavio is enjoying himself.

"Flavio! What are you doing? You're being rude for no reason," Kim nudges him. "

What's the matter? A bit of fun with the floppy green ones can never hurt," he grins.

"We're not floppy. At least not yet," the lettuce corrects Flavio's words.

"Well, it's not far off. Just wait till somebody forgets you in the bottom of their fridge," Flavio laughs.

"Why would somebody forget me in the fridge? And anyway, if I can get forgotten, the same can happen to you. You don't expect to live forever in a fridge box do you?" the lettuce replies.

"It's very unlikely that a speciality like me gets left in the back of the fridge. And if the impossible should occur for some non-existent reason, there's nothing to worry about. We stay good for quite some time. No stress whatsoever!" Flavio explains with a perky smile.

"Sea-sick boy. I wouldn't feel so sure about that. I saw how quickly your colour can change," a bright orange vegetable from the crate in front of them joins the discussion.

"What are you talking about?" Flavio barks at the pointy vegetable.

"Ha, we can see very well in the dark. We spent all our growth time in the earth's ground and have therefore developed advanced vision in darkness. We saw you, my friend. You're the complaining pepper who was rolling all over the place like a baby. So, no reason to get big headed, just because you are on safe ground now. We know!" the pointy vegetable grins.

"Marple, what are they? Look at them, their colour is lovely," Apollo asks admiringly.

"Oh, sorry. We didn't introduce ourselves, did we? We are carrots," the carrot politely smiles.

"Obviously you are. You and green elephant ear will make a good salad together," Flavio counters, feeling a little hot.

"I'm really sorry! We're not all that rude," Marple apologises. "We are Pimientos de Padrón, from the valley of hopes and dreams," she proudly adds.

"Come on Marple, this is a waste of our time. We don't need to communicate with these other ones. What for? We're not going to end up on the same plate. We're a dish of our own," Flavio complains.

"So what? That doesn't mean we can't be nice. And anyway, you're chatting with them non-stop." Marple roles her eyes at him.

"I can only apologise. He's a MARVELLOUS-ME soul. What more can I say?" Marple smiles apologetically, excusing Flavio. "So where does your destiny lie?" she kindly asks, trying to change the heated subject.

"I've been told that we are off to the Borough Market in central London," the carrot politely replies. "That is, if one of the market stall owners bids for us today in the warehouse over there," says the carrot, pointing to a large building on the other side of the harbour.

"We don't doubt it though. Look at us! We're perfect carrots with a lovely colour. And even our green bushy hat has been left on. Doesn't it make a wonderful colour mix?" a second carrot chimes in.

"You surely are. We'll make a lovely bouquet of colours, lying next to each other," Kim smiles, stroking her well-shaped body.

"What will happen to you once you've been bought by a human?" Apollo shyly asks.

"We will be washed, peeled and then eaten," the second carrot smiles.

"Ouch, peeled?" Winston pulls a pained expression.

"Yeah, that's the ticket we got unfortunately. But nothing comes from nothing!" the first carrot pulls a similar expression.

"We're not always peeled though. Some eat us just the way we entered this world. All natural! No poisonous chemicals involved. There are a lot of vitamins in our skin, you know," the second carrot tells them.

"And then what?" Apollo wants to know.

"We become part of the human who eats us. We're especially good for their eyesight," the second carrot gleams.

"Nearly the same as us?" Apollo screeches in surprise.

"Not if we make it first," Flavio points out. "That's why we're appetisers. We come first!" he warns them, showing his index finger. "And if some of you make it through, I don't mind if you enlighten my night vision," he adds with a digging look.

The ship's workers come back with more crates and stack other Pimientos de Padrón on top of them. Inescapably, the peppers are back in the dark again.

Once among themselves again, Marple kicks Flavio.

"Why are you arguing with carrots and lettuce? It's silly! We are a speciality and should behave accordingly. There's no need to be rude. We're not in competition," Marple insists.

"As usual, you are so boring," Flavio grunts.

"Oh, I'm sorry. But I don't see the point of wasting my energy. We're better off exchanging and learning from each other than just arguing over grotesque, want-to-be facts. Calm down!" Marple snaps.

"You calm down!" replies Flavio, hitting back with angry eyes. "If I had some carrots right now, I could see where to kick you," Flavio boasts.

The engine of a forklift truck interrupts their fight. Two metal protrusions slide into the wooden pallet and gently lift them from the ground. They are swirled around and swiftly driven across the harbor to the large warehouse on the other side.

"Oh, this is fun. This is a kind of machine, isn't it?" says Apollo, enjoying the ride. "I know we're not flying, but it feels a little like it, because we're up in the air," he gleams.

"A little maybe. But it's not like that for the driver. You know that, right?" Winston carefully asks.

"Oh, yes. But I'm still enjoying it. Machines are definitely my thing," Apollo admits, making Marple laugh and forget her dispute with Flavio.

The warehouse smells of fresh fish and vegetables. In the middle of the bustling room, the forklift unloads their crates and quickly turns and leaves the room. Through the handle holes of their crate, they can see humans rushing round, sticking labels on all the boxes.

"The bidding will soon start," Marple remarks, rubbing her chin.

"Borough Market, here we come," Kim purrs, shaking her hair. "Borough Market," Apollo repeats. "We have arrived on the ground of our future. We are here! We're home!" Apollo cheers.

While the peppers wait for the bidders to arrive, their hopes and dreams stretch out over London's most renowned vegetable market. That is where they will first see their human-to-be. Quietly they pray that their dreams will be fulfilled and that fate will be good to them.

The invisible protecting hand of the land of the Pimientos de Padrón stretches itself further, and touches the place to be of every passionate London chef and amateur cook. The Borough Market of the hopes and dreams of Pimientos de Padrón.

Our communal spirit 13

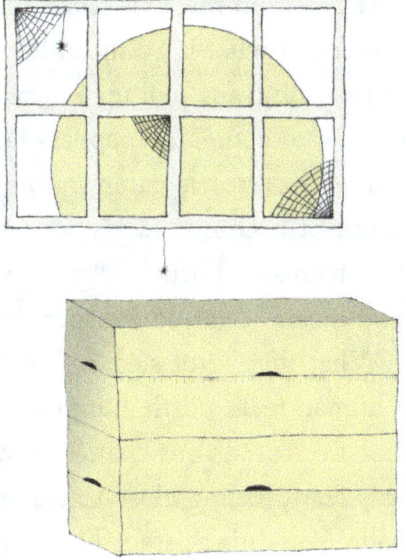

It's like watching a film in fast-forward mode. Forklifts drive in, unload crates and drive out again. Workers rush around, labelling freight and pushing the heavy loads into position. Folding tables and chairs are made ready. The warehouse fills while its dusty glass windows colour with the welcoming orange of the rising sun.

By 5:30 a.m., the warehouse is fully packed with fresh goods. In a moment of silence, the bidders get ready to start. A smell of fresh coffee from thermos flasks fills the room and spikes the excitement of what is going to happen.

Outside, the first minivans pull up and park. In a state of anxiety about what is to come, the peppers lie stiff and still.

"Marple, what if a carrot is eaten before we are? What then? Is our chance of becoming a higher living being gone forever? Will my dreams be buried?" Apollo wants to know.

"What do you mean?" Marple whispers back.

"You know! What the carrot said before. What if we are bought and the human feels a little hungry on the way home and decides to eat a carrot? Is our chance then gone forever?" Apollo repeats his fears, feeling close to tears.

"Oh no, Apollo. You didn't listen. The carrots are needed. They are here for the human's good eye vision. We all serve different purposes. Before and after their consumption of us, they still need more nutrition to stay strong and healthy," says Marple, calming him.

"There is a food hierarchy, you know. We are lucky to be filling the top boxes - we're a speciality," Flavio grins.

"What Flavio is saying is that we all have our raison d'être, our right to exist," Kim adds, enjoying using a little French language once again.

"It looks like you are back in your role, Kim," Winston proudly smiles. "Mais oui, sûrement," she purrs, nudging Winston.

"Now it all starts again," Marple complains, rolling her eyes at the pair of them. "Anyway, Apollo, don't worry. All kinds of nutrition serve to advance the human's mind and body in different ways. We are just very fortunate to not only nourish the skin, flesh and bones. We have a more advanced purpose," Marple smiles at him.

"So what would that be?" wonders Apollo.

"Hopes and dreams, of course. We will fulfil hopes and dreams," Marple answers, looking at him a little worried.

"Oh yes! Yes, hopes and dreams," Apollo repeats, a little unsure of himself.

"It's probably just the early morning hour and the excitement," Winston comments dryly.

The first bidders make their way through the stacked crates and start haggling with the sellers. Within minutes, the acoustic level in the room rises beyond measure.

Through the handle holes of their crate, they can see a gentleman dressed in smart, brown cords, a waxed jacket, and matching hat, studying their label. His pink and white striped scarf is neatly bound to a loose knot. With a silver pen in his hand, he runs through his little notepad, every now and then stopping and tapping one of the listed items with the ballpoint.

"I would like to see one of the pimientos," he asks the seller, a young lady dressed in worn-out blue jeans and a purple university jumper. Her hair is brushed into a practical ponytail and she is warming her fingers with a hot tin cup of coffee. She places the cup down on the table in front of her and turns to the stacked crates. Standing on her tiptoes, she balances and reaches for a pepper.

"No, no. Not one from the top. Show me one from the middle," the brown-cord gentleman politely requests.

"Okay, no problem, one of the middle ones," she repeats, unfazed. Her hand runs down the stack and comes to rest in front of their box. Marple holds her breath and ducks back, trying to escape the fingers that are entering through the handle hole. Her fingers dig into the peppers and quickly choose two.

"Hey!" Flavio screams angrily. But it's too late, and the young lady doesn't hear his voice anyway. Flavio and another pepper are pulled out of the box by their stems.

"Teach him right for always being at the front or on top," says Winston, dryly commenting on the scene.

"Winston! That was Flavio!" Kim protests in shock. "How can you be so cruel?" she blinks, close to tears.

"Oh don't worry, I'm sure he'll work his way out of it. He always does," says Winston smoothly.

"What are they doing?" Apollo asks anxiously, afraid to look by himself. Carefully, Marple leans closer to the handle holes to have a look. The young lady hands the two defenceless peppers to the smartly dressed man, who examines the peppers in his hand. Approvingly, he looks at them in the light. And then it happens. Without any warning or hesitation, he snaps one of the peppers in the middle and examines the inside.

"Eek!" Marple screams, ducking back.

"What's the matter?" Winston asks in shock, catching Marple.

"Arrgh, he has snapped one of the peppers in two. Just like that!" she pants.

"What do you mean?" asks Winston, not believing her words. He moves to the front to get a better view.

"Oh God, please! I feel faint," Kim sobs, waiting for Winston to provide them with more information.

And there it is, in full view. Winston watches the man examining the inside of one of the peppers. He holds it up to his nose and sniffs.

"Yep, they look good! I'll take these boxes," he nods and drops the broken pepper to the ground.

"Is Flavio still alive?" asks Kim anxiously, almost losing her voice.

"I think so. He's still holding the plumper pepper. That can only be Flavio," says Winston, commentating on the scene in front of him.

"What's he doing with him? Is he going to eat him?" Apollo asks innocently.

"No! He won't eat an uncooked pepper," Marple assures him, pushing herself back to the handle hole. "He still has him in his hand," Winston goes on commentating.

The young lady in the purple university jumper pulls out a notepad from the back pocket of her jeans, places a black sheet between two white ones and starts making some notes. While she does this, the man looks around the storage area and rubs Flavio as though he was holding a coin between his thumb and index finger.

"He's getting a massage," Winston chuckles, not noticing Kim's deadly look.

"Here you go," the young lady smiles after a minute to the gentleman and hands him a piece of paper. "Could you fill in your billing address, please?" she politely asks. The gentleman looks at her for a second, tosses Flavio into the crate on top of the stack, takes the paper and lays it on the table between them.

"He's thrown Flavio into the top crate," Marple gasps.

"Are you sure? Is he really back in a crate," Kim cries, and claps her hands to her cheeks.

"Well, I don't know if he made it, but he certainly flew in that direction," Marple blinks.

"Knowing him, he's surely back in one of the crates," says Winston, trying to calm them down.

"Do you really think so?" Kim asks.

"Yes, I'm sure! My being would else be in vain," smiles Winston shyly.

"I wish he was here," Kim whispers.

"Me too! I wish he was here, too," Apollo joins in with her mood.

"We'll have to quickly get used to this. Our time of shared travel will come to an end soon. We'll all be heading different ways. Each of us will go down his or her own path of destiny," Marple warns, looking down to her feet.

"Can't we just all go into the same shopping bag and be eaten by the same person? That way we could always stay together," asks Apollo, with hope sparkling from his eyes.

"We could, Apollo, but that would mean we wouldn't fulfil our dreams, our very own inner destiny. The reason why we were born to this world. In the long term, we wouldn't achieve full happiness," Marple replies and rubs his hand.

"I would be happy to stay with all of you," Apollo sulks.

"I know! So would I. But our dreams are totally different. We want different things to happen in our lives-to-be. Within our new surroundings we'll find new friends, lovers and most importantly, soul mates," Marple smiles.

"That doesn't mean we can't meet in our new lives and be friends and family again," Apollo protests. "No, it doesn't! Absolutely! Who knows what happens once we've been transformed. I've heard that the world is a village. If that's so, the possibility of us meeting again is high," Marple encourages him.

"We will meet again!" Apollo decides.

With a jerk, their crates are lifted and carried to the entrance of the warehouse. The smartly dressed gentleman shakes hand with the young lady and follows his purchase. Outside, they are quickly carried to a white delivery van and carefully stored in the back.

The car's smooth engine purrs into life and they swiftly drive out of the harbour onto an empty road. The intoxicating city is still sleeping while they travel through the narrow streets of London.

The Pimientos de Padrón are wide awake though. Even though they can't watch the city passing them by, they know they have arrived in a very special place. A place of character and style. A city that lives and breathes, and cannot be stuck in just one drawer. A base that opens the doors to the world and offers them all their dreams on a silver plate.

In the valley of Pimiento de Padrón, Mother Earth smiles with happiness. It knows with certainty that its peppers have arrived in the city of their dreams.

Finding the now 14

After a short drive, they arrive at Borough Market. Their crates are quickly carried through arches, and into the market area. The market stands are already built up and are spread over the whole area. Stall owners are rushing back and forth, unpacking items and placing them in the perfect position on their tables.

Their crates are deposited behind a large stand in the middle of the market. Large wicker baskets line the stand, some already filled with potatoes, chillies and colourful, sweet paprika peppers.

"Henry!, Susan!" the smartly dressed gentleman shouts. The man and woman who were busily preparing the large stand look-up. "Here, look! I bought some fresh Pimientos de Padrón. Their juicy green colour will look wonderful between the red and yellow paprika," he smiles.

"They definitely will," Susan agrees, lifting one of the crates and peering inside. "There's an empty basket over there," she points.

"Henry, can you help me shift the paprika and potatoes to make space?" she asks.

"Sure, where do you want them?" Henry eagerly asks.

While the two of them rearrange the wicker-baskets, the Pimientos de Padrón try to get a look at the surroundings.

"We're going into a basket," Apollo proudly announces.

"Luckily we're not in the top crate. I wouldn't want to be at the bottom of the basket," Winston remarks.

"Flavio is in the top one," Kim screeches.

"He'll make his way to the top, as usual," Marple dryly reassures. "I'm more worried that we could get stuck in the middle," she continues, pulling a face. "What do you think, Winston? How many crates will fit into that basket?" she asks.

"Hmm, it doesn't look too deep. For sure they're not going to fit us all in," replies Winston.

"Yes, well, let's hope we make it to the top. I don't want to be somewhere in the middle and every time the top layer is sold, they pour new peppers on top of us," worries Marple.

"What do you think, Tom?" Susan asks the smartly dressed gentleman.

"That looks right. Let me hand you a crate," Tom offers, putting down his coffee cup. "I think we'll fit three to four boxes," Susan smiles. "Here you go! Number one and two." Tom hands her two crates that she quickly tips into the basket.

"Okay, one more," Susan requests.

"At what position are we?" Kim asks.

"I am not sure. Somewhere in the middle," worries Marple.

The lid above them is lifted and bright light floods their crate.

"Ahh, my eyes," Kim cries.

"We're number four," Marple shouts, ignoring Kim's cry. "That means we could be very lucky or very unlucky," Marple carries on, trying to quickly get used to the light.

"Please let there be space for us. Please, please!" Apollo prays.

"What do you think? One more?" Susan asks, looking up to Tom while pushing the peppers around in the basket.

"Yeah, let's do one more. It looks better if the baskets are close to overflowing." Tom nods and passes her the next crate.

"Yes! Yes! This is us!" Marple celebrates, waving her arms back and forth.

"Hold on, Marple," Winston grabs on to her arm. "You don't want to go tumbling out of our box right at this moment," he warns with a smile. Before Marple can calm down, they are poured into the wicker-basket.

"Wow, is everyone all right?" Marple gasps, pushing a pepper on top of her to the side.

"I'm here, Marple," says Apollo, pushing himself closer.

"We're here too," Kim waves, holding on to Winston. "Oh good! Good!" Marple sighs. "We're on top! This is amazing," she smiles, enjoying the view.

"What else do we have?" Henry asks Tom.

"I have some ginger, red beans, baby asparagus and artichokes. Oh, and you have to see these wonderful glass bottles of sea salt I found," Tom goes on, as the three start working on the next load.

"How long until we're bought?" Apollo asks with sparking eyes.

"Looking at that clock up there, the market must open in about thirty minutes," replies Marple, quickly analysing the situation.

*****

Beneath them, some of the peppers start to move.

"What's going on? Keep still!" a pepper complains.

"Oi, get out of my way," a familiar voice grumbles. Peppers are pushed aside, and the top, outside layer is moved around in a circle. In the middle, an inward leading crater opens and some of the peppers, unable to hold on, tumble towards the opening.

"What's this?" an anxious pepper shouts.

"Hold on and keep calm!" Winston orders.

"This is like quicksand," Marple adds with worry. Some kicking and shouting is going on in the centre of the crater. A redheaded pepper bobs up and down and wildly swings his arms around.

"For God's sake! Get out of my way. I'm only getting my birthright back. I made it possible that you all were bought. Without me we wouldn't be here. Show some respect!" the angry redheaded pepper demands.

"Oh God, that can only be Flavio," Winston sighs.

"Definitely!" Marple agrees.

"Flavio! Flavio!" Kim screeches for joy and jumps towards the opening.

"Hey, stay here!" Winston shouts and just manages to catch her foot. "Whatever his birthright is, you have one too," he adds, criticising her outburst.

"But it's Flavio! I have to help him up," an annoyed Kim tries to wriggle her foot free of Winston's clutch.

"It's not your duty to pave his path. He'll make his own way. We all have to," Winston grumbles angrily, and pulls her back.

Flavio pushes one last pepper aside and climbs up the crater. The opening closes behind him, followed by grumbling and angry looks. But Flavio doesn't mind, he doesn't even seem to notice the disapproving, angry bullets flying in his direction.

"Hey guys, I'm back!" Flavio smiles, brushing down his body. The red colour in his face slowly evens out.

"You are, indeed!" Winston dryly greets him.

"Flavio! You're back! You don't know what this means to me," says Kim, blinking lavishly.

"I'm so happy too! It just wasn't the same without you." Apollo smiles sincerely.

"Well, I just had to save the world and make sure we ended up here," boasts Flavio, and stretches his arms out as if the market belonged to him.

"We're really happy you made a good impression, and I'm glad you were tossed back into a crate. Just think what happened to the other pepper!" says Marple, putting his statement into perspective. Flavio just snorts, folds his arms behind his head and leans back.

"Marple, look! The first visitors are coming," Apollo nudges.

"Oh yes, you're right! Get into position everybody. Our future is coming!" Marple excitedly commands.

"Marple, I know we're here to achieve a higher goal. We are the future generation. But what about the now?" Apollo whispers.

"What do you mean by the now?" Marple asks.

"Well, you know. We are now in the now and isn't it nice and worth living for? I mean, being with you on this adventure. Right now, lying next to you, watching the market come alive and feeling the excitement make my mouth water like a grain of salt on my tongue. I wouldn't want to be anywhere else." Apollo smiles with tears of happiness gathering in the corner of his eyes. "Just think of the ones we lost on our journey! Clark… he stayed back to secure generations to come. The pepper that gave himself to the dog to protect us. Or the sick pepper that chose a life under the waves of the great ocean. They didn't consciously know about their future. The future is something we don't yet have and the past is gone, which makes the present so much more important. Don't you think so?" Apollo blinks.

"You're right, Apollo, I also wouldn't want to be anywhere else. And you are also right about the future. We all have our own dreams and claims, but we don't know what will really happen. Life has taken some unexpected turns for some of us, hasn't it," Marple agrees. "I agree with you, Apollo. To the now!" Marple pretends to hold a glass and stretches it towards

Apollo. Apollo does the same and clinks his imaginary glass against Marple's. Both smile.

"Hey, we want to say cheers too," Winston joins in. Winston, Kim and Flavio hold their air-glasses up, and together they all toast themselves.

*****

Some dark jeans come close to their basket. Above them they can see a middle-aged man with dark hair, studying the vegetables on show.

"How can I help you?" Susan smiles. "We have some lovely Pimientos de Padrón today," she gestures to the basket.

"Hmm," the man ponders. "How do you prepare them?" he asks.

"Quite easy. You just fry them in hot oil for a few minutes. Sprinkle some good salt on them and they are ready to enjoy," Susan explains. The man glances around the stand. "It's a Spanish speciality," Susan adds, trying to convince him.

"I'm not sure. I'll definitely have some of that ginger and two sweet red peppers," he decides, rubbing his chin.

"Tsst, he is going for sweet peppers and ginger. I can't believe this," Flavio hisses.

Susan packs the red, sweet peppers and ginger into a paper bag.

"Anything else?" she politely asks. "Hmm, okay, give me just a handful of the... what did you call them?" he gestures to their basket.

"Pimientos de Padrón." Susan smiles.

"Yes, exactly! A handful of those, just to experiment," he smiles back.

"He isn't having me. He cannot even remember our name for thirty seconds," grunts Flavio in disgust.

Susan's hand comes down towards them and digs into the peppers. Flavio, Winston, Kim, Apollo and Marple instinctively move aside and escape her fingers.

"Here you go. What do you think? Is this enough for an experiment?" she asks with a wink.

"Yeah, that'll be fine. If I like them, I know where to find you," the man nods, takes his purchase and moves on.

Next, two pairs of long legs walk up to their stand. A beautiful dress covers the lady from the knees upwards. The other is wearing a pair of neat looking shorts.

"Oh, look Mum. Pimientos de Padrón! Now, they would be easy and quick to make. What do you think?" the younger lady wearing the shorts asks.

"That's an idea. They look nice and fresh," the mother agrees.

"How can I help you, ladies," Susan gleams. "We are just eying-up your Pimientos de Padrón," the mother admits.

"We are having an event with some people from all over. I don't even know most of them," the young lady pulls a face. "We need some easy-to-make finger food," she carries on.

"Well, you can't go wrong with Pimientos de Padrón. Everybody loves them. We also have some wonderful sea salt to go with them, if you like." Susan holds up a bottle with a cork lid. "That sounds good. What do you think, Mum," the young lady turns to her mother.

"Yes, lets go with that," the mother nods. "Can you please fill us a large bag and we will take one bottle of the salt," the mother confirms.

"Oh, oh, this is going to be us," whispers Kim, widening her eyes.

Susan moves around the stand and kneels down next to the Pimientos de Padrón. Her hands quickly dig into the peppers. Marple and Apollo are picked up and poured into the paper bag. Winston, Kim and Flavio follow with the next handful.

"We are together in the bag. Just as I wished for," Apollo sparkles.

"We are! And off to a party," Marple giggles.

More peppers are poured on top of them. Then the bag is closed. The brown paper is soft and only lets very little light in. Cheek to cheek, the peppers lie next to each other and try to catch the words spoken in the world outside. Their bag is laid down in a basket or something similar. They can hear coins exchanging hands. Then they are lifted into the air and carried off.

The two women chat on and visit some other stands, but the peppers cannot make out what they are saying or where they are going. They are left no choice but to patiently wait and trust

*****

Some time later, it must be close to lunchtime, the peppers arrive on the kitchen table of a large townhouse. The kitchen's surface is a cool marble, which takes away the heat of the midday sun. The young lady wearing shorts sits on the table and turns the paper bag upside down. The peppers tumble onto the marble surface.

"Nancy, look! We got some Pimientos de Padrón and sea salt," the young lady marvels, looking down at the peppers.

"Oh, good. They will make a treat," Nancy nods.

"How is it going, Nancy?" the mother asks, entering the kitchen.

"Everything is just fine. I've got the mini pies ready, the vegetable sticks are done, the cake has been delivered and so have the drinks. Salmon rolls, triangle sandwiches, mozzarella and cherry sticks and cured ham with melon are in the fridge," Nancy proudly finishes her list.

"Oh that's good. You're such a star! I don't know what I'd do without you. So we only need to prepare the cheese cakes and those Pimientos de Padrón?" the mother asks.

"Yes, but I would wait until shortly before the guests arrive to do those. We don't want them to be cold," Nancy recommends.

"Good, so we better get freshened-up and ready." The mother smiles and leaves the room.

"It'll be a lovely welcoming party. Don't worry, my dear." Nancy pats the young lady's leg.

"Yeah. It's just strange when you don't know anybody. I find it so exhausting to find talking points," the young lady sulks.

"Well, they're all neighbours and work colleagues of your mum and dad. You can ask them for some recommendations, some insider tips about London. Let them do the talking. Everyone likes to talk about their experiences," Nancy smiles reassuringly. "Now then, you'd better go and get ready," Nancy orders. The young lady sighs, jumps from the counter and leaves the room.

With one stroke of the arm, Nancy sweeps the peppers into a colander and sprinkles fresh water over them.

"Ooh, a wash," Kim oozes.

"Haven't we already done this?" Apollo asks.

"We've been through many stations since then. Take the chance and give yourself a rub," Marple grins.

Carefully, Nancy, slips her fingers under the peppers and gently turns them on all sides, while humming a song.

"Ah, this is nice," Flavio groans, closing his eyes.

"Get yourself together," Marple cannot suppress.

The water is turned off and the peppers are poured onto some white kitchen paper to dry.

"There you go. Make sure you dry nicely. We don't want the oil to spit now, do we," Nancy warns the peppers. Without waiting for an answer, she goes back to humming her song and leaves the kitchen. The peppers are on their own.

"She spoke to us. Did you notice, Marple?" Apollo excitedly observes.

"That's what they call talking to themselves. I mean, yes, she is talking to us, but not because she thinks we can actually hear her," Marple explains.

"Yes, yes, of course," Apollo looks away to hide his excitement and wipes away a drop of water.

"But she is right, you know. We'd better make sure we're dry. These beautiful looking water pearls can become dangerous. I mean, they don't endanger our path of being eaten. But they'll sting our skin terribly mixed with the hot oil," Kim warns, rubbing her back on the smooth, kitchen paper.

"So this is it! Here we are, ready to go. I've enjoyed our journey, my friends," Marple blinks.

"I have too! And I'm so happy we've made it all the way together," Apollo beams. "Who do you think these people are that are coming to this welcoming event?" he continues.

"I don't know. But what I do know is that we are very fortunate, as there will be many different characters. We all have the chance to find our perfect human," Marple smiles happily. "And maybe we will stay neighbours or somehow attached work-wise," Apollo adds.

"I don't know. My human must only be here in this country as a guest. I will be off south tomorrow. Maybe I have a holiday residence here," Flavio assures them.

"I think I'll be the star performer of this evening. I'm sure they have a show planned. Get ready for the soul of MARVELLOUS-ME," Kim performs.

"Do you think so? I didn't hear anything like that?" Marple wonders.

"Of course they do. Look at the house," Kim stabs her with her look.

"Winston, don't worry, they will surely have some security guards on watch. You're future is secured," Flavio chuckles.

"Yeah, you would like that, wouldn't you! This area feels right for Marple and me, our soul of CLARITY will be fed by humans with deep knowledge. I can feel it!" Winston defends his source. "And you don't worry, Apollo. A soul of INNOCENCE will always find his home," Winston smiles.

The black hand of the kitchen clock slowly moves across its white background, and faintly ticks every minute.

About an hour later, Nancy comes back to the kitchen. She has changed into a fresh dress and her hair is combed. She turns the oven on and slides a dish with cheese cakes inside. Then she turns on the chip pan. While waiting for the oil to heat up, she studies the salt and loosens the lid.

"Oh my God. We will be due any minute," Kim panics.

"I recommend you all go into yourselves. Try to connect to your inner soul as deeply as you can. Let the ancient energy flow through you and make yourself big. Picture the life awaiting you. It'll make the transition easier. It's not going to be nice, but we will survive," says Marple, encouragingly.

In the distance, the chip pan starts to sizzle. Nancy is reading a list that she holds in her hand.

Apollo looks up to Marple with a worried look. "Close your eyes. You don't need to see any more for the moment. You'll soon open your eyes to a new life. Think of that. It will be okay," Marple looks him deep in the eye and stretches out her hand towards him. Apollo clutches her hand and closes his eyes.

A few seconds later, the chip pan's ready light pings on, startling Nancy.

"Oh! Okay, okay. I'm coming," she says, talking to herself, and lifts up the white kitchen paper.

Warm air brushes the peppers' skin and a smell of fresh olive oil fills the air. Below them, the hot oil bubbles and sizzles. The heat is unbearable, as if they were hanging over a volcano that is ready to erupt. Even though still wrapped in kitchen paper, the peppers can feel a thousand olive tongues jump up towards them, slashing from side to side like whips. Every blow will scar their shiny skin, but change their life forever.

Apollo presses Marple's hand one more time before Nancy tips the white kitchen paper.

In the land of the hopes and dreams of Pimientos de Padrón, the valley screeches, feeling the immense pain of their children's transformation. But also because it knows that the real journey now begins.

Transformation 15

A young, pretty girl is led into the Parker's kitchen. There are still some boxes standing around with all kinds of souvenirs from faraway places. Places where the Parkers lived, before moving to central London this month. Their new home in Marylebone is spacious for London. The view of some green trees through the windows is a wonderful contrast to the too-white inside of the house.

"Jade!" Nancy wakens the young girl from her daydream. "Dear, this is the kitchen. I have prepared all the dishes that need to be served," Nancy explains, studying the too-slim girl.

"Oh, okay. I understand," Jade smiles, letting her hand travel across the fine material of the curtains lining the window.

"Here is an apron to wear. Thank you for wearing a white blouse," Nancy smiles.

"Yes, of course," Jade smiles, and places her leather jacket onto one of the boxes.

"So, what do you do other than supporting catering events?" Nancy asks.

"Hmm, I study art at King's College," Jade whispers, and draws a half circle across the floor with her pointed toe.

"What are those?" Jade asks, pointing to the fried peppers.

"Those are Pimientos de Padrón. A Spanish tapas speciality. Just a minute, I'll salt them. Then you must try one," Nancy crumbles fresh sea salt over the plate of peppers. "There you go. Try one!" Nancy orders.

"Okay," Jade's slim fingers grab a pepper and pops it into her mouth.

"Uhh, that's hot," she complains, waving her hand in front of her mouth.

"Hot? They've been out of the oil for a couple of minutes. It can't be that bad," says Nancy, wrinkling her forehead.

"No, no, I don't mean that kind of hot. I mean it's a spicy pepper," gasps Jade, after swallowing the pepper down.

*****

Jasmine studies the invitation to the Parker's welcoming party one more time.

"This must be it," she comments, looking at the house number and the invitation.

"Well then, ring the bell," John encourages her. Jasmine rings the bell and turns to her two grown-up children with a smile.

"It's nice that you are coming along," she smiles.

"Their daughter must be about your age," John adds.

Mrs Parker opens the door. "Hi there. I'm Silvia. It's so lovely that you could come. Please come in," she smiles genuinely.

"Thank you, this is so kind of you. I'm Jasmine. This is my husband, John. Our daughter, Sophia and our son,

Finlay. They're both at Oxford University," Jasmine proudly introduces.

"Oh wonderful. I must introduce you to my daughter. She's currently looking at universities. I'm sure she'll be interested to hear about Oxford."

Mrs Parker guides them through the entrance and living room, and out onto the open terrace. A beautiful, blue, wisteria is in full bloom on one of the walls and a wonderful scent fills the air.

"Please feel at home," Mrs Parker smiles, and waves to Jade. "Jade will help you get some drinks," Mrs Parker offers. "Oh here, my daughter... Willow. Willow, this is Jasmine, John, Sophia and Finlay. Sophia and Finlay are at Oxford University," Mrs Parker nods, introducing everyone to her daughter.

"Excuse me, can I offer you some red or white wine," Jade shyly asks, noticing that Finlay is studying her.

"Oh, and you have to try some of these," says Willow, gesturing to the Pimientos de Padrón that Jade has placed on a table. "We bought them at the market today," Willow adds excitedly. Sophia and Finlay pick up a pepper each.

*****

Maurizio is sitting on one side of the Parker's terrace with his cousin Silvio.

"This is so boring. Why are we here?" Silvio persistently looks at this cousin. "I'm not over every day, you know. I'm in

London and what do you do, you take me to your neighbour's house-warming party," Silvio grunts.

"Mio amico, we won't stay long. I just want to see who my new neighbours are. You'd do the same. Actually, back home you only hang with the family and neighbours," says Maurizio, trying to calm him down.

"Mai, that is something else," Silvio complains and gets up from his chair. "So please make sure you get to know these Parkers so that we can leave. You'll find me over there, where the food is."

Silvio shakes his head and makes his way over to the buffet. The plate of Pimientos de Padrón catches his eye first.

*****

Lucian dries his hands on the soft towel in the guest bathroom. He takes a deep breath before he unlocks the door. He is a little shy, and is very sensitive to any change of energy. But he has come to meet people, and that's what he'll do. He only needs a second to convince his inner self.

He only moved to Marylebone a month ago. His parents' money made the move easy for him, as a young man of his age, wanting to become an explorer, couldn't normally afford this area. But he doesn't take advantage of his parent's wealth, and he's determined to pay back every penny as soon as possible. His aircraft engineering studies will finish in less than a year.

For a moment, he watches himself exhale and combs a loose strain of his too-long hair back into place.

"Here we go," he whispers to himself, and opens the door.

In the living room, he can't help noticing the black and white pictures of faraway places, in expensive looking wooden frames. The Parkers seem to like to travel, he thinks, admiring the photographs. One picture is slightly slanted. With one finger, he pushes the lower side upwards until the frame hangs straight. That's better, he thinks, and smiles to himself.

Some people are sitting in the living room and are casually chatting. They haven't noticed him. He doesn't feel comfortable about joining them on the sofa, so he makes his way to the terrace.

The air outside is warm and welcoming.

"Can I offer you a glass of wine," asks a slim girl wearing a white blouse and black apron. She is balancing a tray with filled glasses on one hand.

"Err, yes, thank you. I will have one of those," Lucian carefully takes a glass of red wine.

"Please help yourself to some finger food over there," she gestures.

"Is there something you'd recommend?" Lucian manages.

"Um, I have only tried the Pimientos de Padrón. I wouldn't recommend them. The one I got was really, really hot," she replies, rolling her eyes and moving on to the next guests.

Studying the buffet, Lucian can't resist. He has to try one of these peppers, even if they could potentially be hot.

A gush of air blows through the Parker's spacious Marylebone home. The long, white curtains gently sway to the soft tunes of Handel's opera, La Resurrezione, Part II, while a dry leaf rustles across the stone floor outside on the terrace. The wind's arms have let it go to rest from its long journey through the land of the hopes and dreams of Pimientos de Padrón.

Epilogue

Imagine an eight-lane motorway in a busy, vibrant city of this world. Hundreds of cars stand in a giant jam. Nothing joins and nothing leaves. Everything stands still. The sun burns down on the steel roof of the cars. The hot air is filled with a mix of overheating rubber, petrol fumes, human sweat and frustration.

In the cars, thousands of people sit and wait. And wait.

Every single person with dreams of his or her own. Thousands of dreams sit in the jam and wait. And wait.

Now change one of these cars.

What would happen?

Is the picture a different one?

Does the world change?

Does the jam vanish?

The world keeps on turning. The moon and the sun rise and set. New souls are born, while others turn to dust. Plants grow and water flows. The life cycle cannot be stopped.

Do dreams cease to exist?

What are you going to do?

What can you do?

And, most important, what are your dreams?

Books by
Katherine Anne Lee

Katherine Anne Lee

"From Dust to Dust and a Lifetime in Between"

ISBN 978-3-9524205-0-8

Growing up in a sheltered dream world in a little English town called Church Stretton, falling in love and getting married. That's the way it should be, a future life that every little girl dreams of. A constant line, a perfect path to follow. That's how all began, shortly before the 1920's.

But that's not how life is, is it? Life's not always fair, and takes turns that are not understandable. And so it was that the first plunge into the deepest dark wasn't far off. An icy cold blizzard hit me, leaving a trail of devastation, only to move on without any explanation.

Life didn't let me go, and getting back to my feet rewarded me with the greatest gift. Rocketing up, I touched the highest mountaintops of love. But life doesn't stand still and moments cannot be frozen. It moves on and tells its own tale.

It wasn't long before I encountered the next fall.

This is my story. This is Mollie's story.

Our yesterday's fortune doesn't belong to us anymore and what's to come tomorrow isn't ours yet. It's only the now that is ours for a short moment.

*****

About "From Dust to Dust and a Lifetime in Between"

The novel, "From Dust to Dust and a Lifetime in Between", is the true story of Mollie Cooke, who was born and grew up in a small town in Shropshire.

During her lifetime, she lived through two world wars, losing her first husband during WWII and having to cope with the pain of early widowhood.

The story tells how she found true love a second time round with her husband Bill, and how their happy life together included the birth of their only child, Sue.

There's the joy of becoming a grandmother to three children, followed quickly by the devastating and unspeakable anguish of losing Sue to cancer, leaving her three grandchildren motherless.

After losing her second husband, Bill, to cancer, Mollie spent the last twenty years of her life living and coping with the degenerative brain disease Alzheimer's.

Mollie's story has been written in the first person by her granddaughter Katherine Anne Lee.

*****

Hello Online
"I was pleasantly surprised to find myself growing increasingly attached to Mollie, the protagonist, as she navigated her way through the highs and lows of life. By the time I finished the novel, it felt as if I had lost a family member of my own."

PurpleMum
"What I found most wonderful about this book was the connection I quickly felt with Mollie despite our different generations. She comes across as a generous, fun lady who is full of love for life. The book is very moving, the way that Katherine writes Mollies dementia, and eventual end is very real and very touching. I finished the book really feeling that I had lost a friend. "

Futures blog
"This book is unlike any I have read before and I liked the fact that I cared about Mollie from the very first page when she asked the reader to call her Mollie – this line instantly gets the reader involved and keeps them reading! It is definitely one of my top books that I read in 2013."

Kirkus Review

"This first-person tale is a loving and heartfelt tribute to Lee's grandmother, drawing upon Mollie's history and bringing her thoughts to life in an upbeat, chatty manner. The book's final third focuses primarily on Mollie's physical and mental decline; the theme of cancer figures predominantly in this section, and it's given voice in an inspiring manner."

Keenly Kristin (US Blogger)

"This book is utterly amazing. I can't tell you how many times I cried, like cried cried. Not teared up but needed a tissue. It's that touching, that gripping, that real. As her debut novel, Katherine Anne Lee should be immensely proud of From Dust to Dust and a Lifetime in Between. It is an exquisite tale and Lee's ability to touch readers' hearts is remarkable. She is a gifted writer, and I will be looking to see if she writes more."

*****

The author's biography

Katherine Anne Lee was born and spent her formative years in Dorset. Aged just five, Katherine and her family moved to Switzerland, where she grew up and continues to live. As a child, Katherine regularly spent summers with her grandparents in a small Shropshire town.

Katherine published her first novel "From Dust to and a Lifetime in Between" in September 2013. Only one year later she released the "Life and Dreams of Pimientos de Padrón".

Katherine's career has included consulting roles in banking and insurance.

More information around Katherine Anne Lee and her books can be found on Facebook, Twitter and her webpage:

www.katherine-anne-lee.com